WILLIAM AND THE POP SINGERS

By the Same Author

"A MESSAGE FROM OUTER SPACE, PERHAPS," SAID MISS THOMPSON. (*See page 183*)

WILLIAM AND THE POP SINGERS

by

RICHMAL CROMPTON

Illustrated by

HENRY FORD

LONDON

GEORGE NEWNES LIMITED

TOWER HOUSE, SOUTHAMPTON STREET

LONDON, W.C.2

First Published 1965

Printed in Great Britain by
Cox & Wyman, Ltd., London, Fakenham and Reading

CONTENTS

For Jill, Kirsty and Robert

I

WILLIAM AND THE POP SINGERS

"HE ought to be here by now," said William.

"We said ten o'clock," said Ginger.

"He's always late when we've got something important to do," said Henry.

They stood in the doorway of the old barn, watching the stile that led from the road into the field.

"We'll start without him if he doesn't come soon," said William.

But already the figure of Douglas could be seen, climbing over the stile and walking slowly across the field.

"You're jolly late," said William as he reached them. "You know we'd planned to build that tree house this mornin' an'——" He stopped, struck by the lugubrious expression on Douglas's face. "What's the matter? Are you in trouble?"

"Trouble?" said Douglas with a mirthless laugh. "I don't think anyone's been in worse trouble since the world began."

"Why?" said William. "What's happened?"

They drew him into the barn and stood round him. A gleam of self-importance broke through the gloom of Douglas's countenance.

"It's the most ghastly trag'dy I've ever had in all my life."

"Well, go *on*. . . . *Tell* us."

"It's Hector's electric razor."

Hector was Douglas's elder brother. He was a youth of high spirit and uncertain temper. Between him and Douglas an intermittent feud had ranged over the years.

"What about the electric razor?" said William.

"I used it."

"Gosh, you don't need to use it *yet*!" said William. "If you thought you were gettin' a moustache it mus' have been choc'late. Choc'late can look jus' like a moustache."

"'Course I didn't think I was gettin' a moustache," said Douglas. "I used it for a plane."

"What d'you mean, a plane?" said William.

"Well, I was makin' a little boat. Jus' a little one an' I wanted a little plane to plane the sides to make 'em nice an' smooth an' I thought an electric razor would be jus' the thing for it, so I borrowed it. I didn't mean to do it any harm. Well, I jus' planed the wood same as people plane a face with it. It only caught on a nail once an' I don't see that could do it any harm, but he said I'd ruined it. He went on at me as if I was a *murderer*. An' he said I'd got to pay for a new one an'—Gosh! It cost two pounds fifteen."

They gazed at him in silent horror.

"But he *can't* do that," said William at last.

"Oh, can't he?" said Douglas bitterly. "You don't know him if you think he can't do that. He's a tyrant, same as the ones in hist'ry. An' you'd think my father'd do somethin' to save me, wouldn't you? Not many fathers'd jus' look on an' watch their son bein' robbed an'—an' *plundered* like that, but mine does. He says that Hector's right an' that it'll teach me a lesson. They're all mad with me, anyway, 'cause one of my arrows made a little hole in the window of the car. It wasn't much of a hole. They needn't have made all that fuss. . . . They're goin' to take half the money for the razor out of my post office savings, but I've got to pay the rest myself. An' it comes to one pound seven an' six. An' I only get two shillin's a week. I jus' shan't have any money for the rest of my life. I'll be payin' it back till I'm an old man. Shouldn't be surprised if it doesn't take all my old-age pension, too. It'll be *years* before I've paid it off."

"Thirteen weeks and a bit," said Henry after a moment's thought.

"Well, that's the same as years," said Douglas. "I mean, it's somethin' you can't see the end of." He sighed deeply. "Why do these things always happen to me? They never do to other people."

"Well, it's no use talkin' about it," said William. "We've jus' got to get that money. We'll put off the tree house till later an' we'll start gettin' the money now."

"How?" said Henry.

"There mus' be ways of gettin' money," said William. "People do get money. . . . Let's think over all the people we know that have got money an' see how they got it."

"There's the Botts," suggested Ginger.

"He makes sauce," said Henry.

"We could make sauce all right," said William, "but I don't s'pose anyone'd buy it. . . . Who else is there?"

"There's Sir Gerald Markham," said Henry. "He got his money from his father."

Douglas produced another mirthless laugh.

"He mus' have a jolly diff'rent sort from the one I've got."

"There's those people that buy things an' sell 'em again," said Ginger.

"We've tried that," said William. "We ended up with less money than we started with."

"You can make money on horses," said Henry, "but I'm not sure how you do it."

"There's doctors an' lawyers," said William, "but you've got to pass exams before you can start bein' one of them an' it'd take too long."

"There's actors," said Ginger. "Some of them get jolly rich. Actresses have furs an' jewl'ry an' poodle dogs an' actors have yachts an' big cigars an' things. They go for holidays to the winter sports an' have parties every night. They must have *masses* of money."

"Yes, but that'd take too long, too," said Henry. "You've got to write a play and then find a theatre and if there's plays on at all the theatres you've got to wait till one's empty and sometimes it's *years*."

"Well, I can't go on havin' no money all that time," said Douglas miserably. "I was goin' to start savin' up to buy roller skates an' I can't wait till I'm an old man for that. You never see an old man on roller skates. I'd jus' look silly on them."

"Of course it was different in the days of strolling players," said Henry thoughtfully.

"What were those?" said William, interested.

"They were actors," said Henry, "but they didn't have a theatre. They jus' went about and acted plays on the greens of villages and places like that and people came round to watch and gave them money."

"Gosh! We could do that," said William, a note of excitement in his voice. "We could do that easy."

"I dunno . . ." said Henry.

"'Course we could," said William. "Now listen. That's what we'll do. We'll be strolling players an' go round the villages actin' plays an' people'll come round to watch us an' give us money an' I bet we get that one pound seven an' six for Douglas in no time."

As usual his optimism communicated itself to the others. Even Douglas's expression lightened somewhat. Only Henry remained thoughtful.

"I don't suppose it'll be as easy as all that," he said.

"Why not?" challenged William.

"Well, we've got to think out a play."

"Gosh, that's easy enough," said William. "There's lots of plays an' anyway we can always make one up."

"There's a play called 'Macbeth'," said Ginger vaguely, "about a king that murdered his relations."

"An' there's one called 'Bluebell in Fairyland'," said Douglas. "They did it at my cousin's school."

"There's the clothes . . ." said Henry.

"We've got lots of dramatic clothes," said William. "Tell you what! We'll all bring dramatic clothes here this afternoon an' see what sort of a play they fit into. . . . Now that's a jolly good idea, isn't it?"

"If it works," said Henry.

"'Course it'll work," said William.

"I've known 'em not to," said Douglas.

They assembled in the old barn early in the afternoon, each carrying his "costume" bundled under his arm.

William had brought a white beard, a pair of

sun-glasses and a hearth-rug with a hole in the middle (the result of a spitting log on the sitting-room fire).

Ginger had brought a space helmet, a plastic breast-plate, and a stethoscope, the sole remaining piece of a doctor's outfit that had been given him at Christmas.

Henry had brought a handleless saucepan, an ancient tweed jacket and the costume that he had worn as Oberon in a school performance of "A Midsummer Night's Dream".

Douglas had brought a gas-mask that had reposed in the box-room since the war, a very old dressing-gown of his mother's (salvaged from the "rummage sack") and a drum that was in fairly good condition as its use had been forbidden within hearing of his family.

"Yes, they're smashing," said William. "Let's put 'em on an' see what we look like in 'em."

They put them on.

William wore his beard and sun-glasses and draped himself in the hearth-rug by the simple means of putting his head through the hole.

Ginger wore his space helmet and breastplate with his stethoscope dangling round his neck.

Little could be seen of Douglas beneath his gas-mask and dressing-gown. His drum was slung over his shoulder.

Still less could be seen of Henry, engulfed in his saucepan, jacket and Oberon draperies.

William inspected the assembled troupe.

"It's jolly fine," he said. There was a faint note of doubt in his voice. "But——"

"It doesn't look like 'Macbeth,'" said Ginger.

"An' it doesn't look like 'Bluebell in Fairyland'," said Douglas.

THEY PUT THEM ON.

"P'r'aps somethin' out of hist'ry . . ." suggested Ginger.

"It doesn't look like anythin' out of hist'ry," said Henry.

"It doesn't look like real people at all," said Douglas.

"*Tell* you what, then!" said William. The note of enthusiasm had returned to his voice. "We won't have it real people. We'll have it people in Space. It doesn't matter how queer we look then 'cause people in Space look jolly queer anyway. . . . Yes, that's what we'll do. We'll have a play about people in Space."

"What play?" said Henry.

"Oh, it's easy enough to think out a play," said William.

"Well, think one out, then," challenged Ginger.

"How can I, when you keep talkin' an' interruptin' all the time?" said William irritably. "I can't poss'bly keep ideas in my head when you keep drivin' 'em out with talkin' an' interruptin'."

"All right," said Henry pacifically. "Go on. Think."

"I've nearly got one already," said William. He drew his features together into their most ferocious scowl. The others watched him in silent expectancy. Gradually the scowl cleared. "I've got it all right now," he said triumphantly. "It's a smashin' one, too. Now listen. . . . There's an old professor—I'll be him 'cause of my beard an' spectacles an' hearth-rug. This hearth-rug's jus' like those gowns that professors wear to show they've passed exams. Well, nearly like 'em, anyway."

"But what does he *do*?" said Ginger.

"What am I goin' to be in it?" said Douglas.

"Can't you be quiet an' *listen*?" said William sternly,

"'stead of drivin' all the ideas out of my head by talkin' an' interruptin' all the time. I'm jus' goin' to *tell* you what he does if only you'd keep quiet for two seconds. . . . Well, he's found a secret ray that goes up an' meets the rays from the moon an' they mix together an' make a sort of powerful magnetic force that draws people shootin' up to the moon without any of that bother with rockets an' capsules, an' he doesn't tell anyone about it 'cause he wants to try it out himself first but he takes a friend with him that knows a bit about Space—that'll be Ginger 'cause of his space helmet—an' they go shootin' up to the moon."

"How can they keep alive there without any oxygen?" said Henry.

"He's invented a special lozenge that keeps 'em alive as long as they go on suckin' it," said William, "an' he takes a big box full of 'em an' they get to the moon an' they find fierce savage monsters there—they'll be Henry an' Douglas—an' these fierce savage monsters are buildin' a machine to destroy the earth an' everyone on it, so Ginger an' me try to stop them but they kidnap Ginger an' keep him prisoner in a deep cave an' I've got to try to rescue him 'cause his lozenges are runnin' out, but they've got a specially fierce savage monster guardin' him with great huge teeth stickin' out of the top of his head, but I've studied hypnotism at this professors' college I've been to an' I hypnotise this monster an' rescue Ginger an' we find a way to blow up the machine they're makin' an' they attack us while we're doin' it an' we have a jolly good fight an' we kill most of them an' the ones that are left make me King an' Ginger Prime Minister an' we go shootin' back to the earth to tell people about it an' we get in the newspapers an' on TV an'—well, that's the end. We can put in a bit more if we like. We'll have to see how long it takes."

"Yes, it's pretty good," said Henry judicially, "but what do we *say*? You've got to say things in a play. You've got to have lines an' learn them."

William dismissed this with a wave of his hand.

"We can make up things to say as we go along," he said. "It's easy to make things up to say as you go along. I bet that's what those strollin' players did. They knew what they'd got to *do* in the play an' they jus' talked about it while they were doin' it. I expect that's what mos' actors do anyway."

"Oh well . . ." said Ginger. "Where are we goin' to start?"

"Where did you say they did those plays, Henry?" said William.

"On village greens, but I expect anywhere'd do."

"There's a village green at Applelea," said William. "Come on. Let's start at Applelea."

The others felt a little bewildered by the speed with which William was marshalling events, but it was a familiar feeling and it never lasted long.

"We'll take our things off now," said William. "We don't want everyone to see them before we start actin'. An' we'll take the short cut to Applelea over the fields."

They divested themselves of their costumes, bundled them under their arms and set off over the fields to Applelea.

The green at Applelea was a fair-sized, squarish stretch of grass with a chestnut tree in the middle and one or two seats ranged at the sides. All the seats were empty except one, which was occupied by an old man and a solidly built, pudding-faced child of about two.

"Lots more people'll come when we get started," said William. "I bet all the people that live here will come *an'* all the people that come along the road in cars."

He approached the seat, cleared his throat and addressed his audience in a loud authoritative voice.

"Lady an' gentleman," he said, "we're strollin' players an' we're goin' to act a smashin' play for you an' when we've finished we'll pass a hat round an' you can give us money an'—an' if you've not got any with you you can go home an' fetch it."

He waited for some response, but his audience continued to stare at him blankly without change of expression.

"Come on," said William impatiently. "Let's dress up. I bet they'll get interested once we start."

"They don't look as if they've got much money," said Douglas.

"Well, other people'll come along," said William. "Let's go behind the tree an' put our things on."

They changed behind the tree and emerged wearing their costumes. Douglas's gas-mask had refused to stay in place, so he wore it as a sort of head piece, and Henry's saucepan showed a tendency to escape the moorings of his ears and lodge itself on his chin . . . but on the whole they made an impressive appearance as they approached the seat again. The old man and the child continued to gaze at them with blank expressionless faces.

"Lady an' gentleman," said William, "the play's jus' goin' to begin. I'm a professor an' I've invented a ray that shoots people up to the moon. An' this play starts

"LADY AN' GENTLEMAN," SAID WILLIAM, "THE PLAY'S JUS' GOIN' TO BEGIN."

with me an' Gin—I mean this man here in the space helmet—gettin' to the moon an' meetin' these fierce savage monsters here"—he pointed to Henry and Douglas—"who live on the moon. They're mad 'cause we've got to the moon, you see, an' they want to know how we got there. Go on, Henry. Say somethin'."

"Whence hast thou come, thou villain?" said Henry, baring his teeth savagely.

"You needn't talk hist'ry," said William. "It's modern times."

"Where have you come from, you old beast?" said Henry.

"Never mind where we've come from," growled

William. "We've come to stop your little game an' break up that machine you're makin' to destroy the earth."

"How dare you!" said Henry. "I'm goin' to push you off the moon . . . an' you can jolly well go back to where you came from."

A scuffle followed which brought all four to the ground.

"You've got it all wrong," said William heatedly. "We don't start fightin' till near the end. You've got to kidnap Ginger first an'——"

"What's all this?" said a voice behind them.

They turned to see a young man in tight black trousers, black jacket, white shirt and sleeked black hair.

"We're strollin' players," said William. "They went about villages, actin' plays an'——"

"I know, I know," said the young man. "Art for art's sake. Those were the days I should have lived in."

William looked at him. There was something vaguely familiar about him but he couldn't think what it was.

"Strolling players . . ." said the young man again, as if the words held some magic for him. He sighed deeply. "I've half a mind to join you."

"Well, there isn't a part for you in this play," said William. "We could put one in, of course. You could be another fierce savage monster."

"No, no," said the young man. "It's too late."

He made a sweeping gesture of despair, strode off to a near-by seat, sat down on it, and dropped his head on to his hands.

William approached him, followed by Ginger, Henry and Douglas.

The old man and the child turned blank expressionless faces in their direction.

"What's the matter?" said William.

The young man raised his head and made another despairing gesture.

"I've wasted my life," he said. "I've cheapened and debased my talent on soul-destroying trivialities."

"What d'you mean?" said William with a puzzled frown.

"I was born out of my time," said the young man. "The age of noise and mechanisation has killed art. I should have been a troubadour, a jongleur, a strolling player."

"Well, why aren't you, then?" said William.

"I've told you. Because I've wasted my life and my talents. But"—he sat upright in his seat and fixed a piercing gaze on William—"why should it be too late?"

"I don't know," said William. "It was you that said it was."

The young man flung an arm in the direction of the road.

"Where does that lead to?"

"Hadley," said William.

"I'll go there. I'll go to Hadley. I'll go where no one knows me and start life afresh—I don't care how humbly. I'd be a farm labourer if I knew a little more about agriculture. But it shall be a life that will redeem the misspent years. I have the soul of a poet, a dreamer, a dramatist."

"Well, I'm one of them," said William, "an' if you'll kin'ly stop talkin' we'll get on with my play. If you want to watch it you can sit down with the rest of the audience"—he pointed to the old man and the child who were now gazing vacantly in front of them—"an' we'll begin."

The young man seemed to notice the equipment of the strolling players for the first time.

"What play is it?" he said curiously.

"It's one I made up," said William, "an' it's a smashin' one. I'll tell you about it an' I bet you'll want to watch it. You needn't bother about payin' money till the end an' if you don't like it you needn't pay."

"An excellent idea," said the young man. "It should be more widely adopted. What's the play about?"

"It's about a professor that found a secret ray," said William, "an' this ray joined with the moonbeams an' sent people shootin' up to the moon an'——"

But the young man wasn't listening. A light had broken out over his face. The drooping corners of his mouth took an upward curve. He sprang to his feet.

"I think you've *got* something there," he said. "I think you've *given* me something. . . . Wait a minute. I must work this out alone."

He strode over the green, crossed the road and disappeared into the wood on the other side.

They watched him in silent amazement for some moments.

"He's mad," said William. "Good thing he didn't turn vi'lent an' start murderin' us! Now come on. Let's do it again from the beginning. Ginger an' me's jus' got to the moon an' we're makin' our way over it, suckin' our lozenges, when we come across this machine Henry an' Douglas are makin' to destroy the earth an' suddenly Henry springs out an' kidnaps Ginger an'——"

The scene ended once more in chaos. William arose breathlessly from the mêlée, straightened his beard and hearth-rug and retrieved his sun-glasses from the ground.

"You keep startin' fightin' too *soon*," he said testily. "Now let's start again an'——"

He stopped. A car had drawn up at the side of the green and three young men were getting out of it. They wore tight black trousers, black jackets and white shirts. Their black hair was sleeked away from their foreheads. One of them carried a brief-case. They approached the Outlaws.

"Have you seen a young man anywhere about here?" said the tallest. "A young man who looks——"

"Like us," said one of the others.

The Outlaws were gazing at them open-mouthed.

"Gosh!" said William. "You're the——"

"Argonauts!" said Henry.

"That's right," said the tallest young man.

"Gosh!" breathed the Outlaws in unison.

"Why, we've *seen* you an' *heard* you on TV," said Henry.

"We've got your photos," said Ginger.

"Out of a packet of Sugar Mints," said Douglas.

"You're Ted."

"You're Johnny."

"You're Pete."

"An' the one that was talking to us is——"

"Chris."

"I *thought* I knew him," said William, "but I couldn't remember. . . ."

"Well, have you seen him anywhere round here?" said Peter.

"GOSH!" SAID WILLIAM. "YOU'RE THE —"
"ARGONAUTS!" SAID HENRY.

"Yes," said William. "He was here jus' a minute ago. He went into the woods over there. You'll catch him up if you hurry."

"No," said Johnny, shaking his head. "We must give him time to work it out of his system."

"Work what out of his system?" said Henry.

"His education," said Johnny with a reverent hush in his voice. "He's educated. It was him that made us call ourselves the Argonauts."

"It's a foreign language," said Ted.

"Out of his education," said Johnny.

"He's our leader," said Pete.

"The brains of us," said Johnny.

"The life and soul of us," said Ted.

"We couldn't get on without him," said Pete.

"But what's *happened*?" said William.

"Why's he gone off?" said Henry.

"It's his education," said Johnny. "Sometimes it comes over him, like, and he's got to work it out of his system."

"He's temperamental," said Ted.

"Excitable," said Pete.

"He's classy," said Johnny. "He's had a classy education and taken classy exams and sometimes it comes over him that he's wastin' his life singin' pop songs and—he's got to work it out of his system."

"He'll go on all right for months and months," said Ted, "and then it comes over him all of a sudden."

"We were staying the night in Fellminster on the way to the Midlands," said Pete. "He was all right last night and this morning it suddenly came over him and he walked out on us."

"Said he was going to start his life afresh and make it more worthy of his talents," said Ted.

"He always says that when it comes over him," said Pete.

"It was partly because of the mail this morning," said Johnny.

"It was late, you see," said Pete, "and he thought he hadn't got any fan-mail and when he doesn't get any fan-mail he thinks he's finished and it comes over him that he's wasted his life. It doesn't last long but it's touch and go while it lasts."

"Temperamental," said Ted.

"Excitable," said Pete.

"It's his education," said Johnny.

"So he walked out on us," said Ted.

"And we couldn't carry on without him," said Pete.

"The mail came after he'd gone," said Ted, "and—Boy!" He held up the brief-case. "He's got the biggest fan-mail he's ever had in his life. I've brought it along with me."

"Well, he's only gone into the wood," said William again. "You'll soon catch him up."

"We'll give him time to get over it," said Ted. "It's no use chasin' him. It only makes him worse, chasin' him."

"But we're due at a show in the Midlands tonight," said Pete. "We'll be dished if he doesn't come back soon."

"Sh!" said Johnny. "I think he's comin'."

The figure of Chris came slowly out of the wood, crossed the road and joined them.

Ignoring the others, he snatched the drum from

Douglas, slipped the strap over his head and began to beat on it with the sticks.

His voice rose, nasal and strident, over the beats of the drum.

"Moon girl, my moon girl,
I'm comin' to you soon, girl,
Shootin' up the moonbeams
'Cos I'm in love with you."

The other three were swinging and writhing their bodies in time with the rhythm.

"Yeah! Yeah! Yeah!" yelled Ted.

"Up the silvery beams, girl.
Where I seen you in my dreams, girl,
Dream girl, dream girl,
I'm in love with you."

The others shouted the words after him. The drum beats were intensified. Their slim bodies squirmed and writhed with snake-like movements.

"Dream girl, dream girl,
I'm in love with you."

"Yeah! Yeah! Yeah!"

"It's a winner, boys!" shouted Chris exultantly, throwing the drum on to the ground. "It's a winner!"

"It'll need a bit of fixing," said Ted, "but it's a winner all right. And—Chris, boy, you're not wasting your life. You're bringing joy to youth an' youth to old age. You're bringin' joy an' hope an' youth to a weary world."

"Yeah! Yeah! Yeah!" yelled Pete.

Chris's face was alight with smiles. There were tears of emotion in his eyes.

"You're right, boy," he said brokenly. "You're sure right."

"He's worked it off," whispered Johnny to William. "He'll be O.K. now for a few months."

"An' look, Chris," said Ted, opening the brief-case. "The mail came after you'd gone an' there's a *pile* of fan-mail for you. An' we got a tip that we'll be in the top ten this week *an'* pretty near the top."

"Oh, boy!" said Chris ecstatically.

"An' we'd better be gettin' on," said Pete, "or we won't make it in time for the show tonight."

"What's this?" said Chris, drawing a small package from the depth of the brief-case.

"An electric razor," said Pete carelessly. "From those people that had your photo usin' it for an advert."

"Well, I've got about six of 'em," said Chris. He turned to the Outlaws. "Any of you kids like an electric razor?"

"Yes, please," said Douglas faintly.

Chris threw it into the air.

"Oo, *thanks*," said Douglas. "*Thanks*."

The Argonauts piled into the car, waved to the Outlaws and drove off.

Dazedly the Outlaws watched them out of sight. Then suddenly they seemed to be galvanized into action. Their solid young bodies writhed and squirmed in ineffectual imitation of the Argonauts. Their voices rose, nasal and strident, against the beating of the drum.

"We've got a 'lectric razor, boys,
We've got a 'lectric razor."

"Yeah! Yeah! Yeah!" yelled Douglas.

"Come on," said William. "Let's go an' start the tree house now."

Shouting, yelling, beating the drum, stopping only to retrieve such of their equipment as dropped from them in their flight, they made their way in running leaps along the road.

> "We've got a 'lectric razor, boys,
> We've got a 'lectric razor."

"Yeah! Yeah! Yeah!"

The raucous young voices died slowly away in the distance.

Peace descended again on Applelea green.

The old man and the child continued to gaze stolidly in front of them.

II

WILLIAM AND THE SCHOOL OF NATURE

"I'VE started writin' another story," said William. His tone held the note of mingled secrecy and importance with which he was wont to refer to his literary activities.

"What's it about?" asked Ginger. "An' stop pushin' your feet down my neck."

"Well, move on to another branch, then. I've got to put my feet *somewhere*, haven't I? I can't turn 'em into air. An' I've got to move 'em about sometimes to give 'em a bit of exercise. It's a jolly excitin' story."

"But what's it *about*?" repeated Ginger, transferring himself at considerable personal risk to a branch beyond the range of William's stout footwear.

The two had started the day at the Browns' house, where Mrs. Brown had set them to tidy the shed in which the logs were kept. When she returned some time later to see how the work was progressing, she found them constructing a space ship out of the logs, the mowing machine, the wheelbarrow, Ethel's bicycle, Mrs. Brown's new umbrella and a vegetable rack filched from the kitchen.

Summarily ejected from the premises, they were now resting from their labours in the apple tree at the bottom of Ginger's garden.

"Go on! Tell me what it's about."

"Well, it's jolly excitin'," said William. "It's about a gang of international diamond smugglers an' they all pretend to be members of a golf club, but really this golf club's a sort of *blind*. It's the headquarters of this smugglin' gang. They only *pretend* to play golf. Really they're smugglin' diamonds all the time."

Ginger considered this in comparative silence as he plunged his teeth into a large red Worcester Pearmain.

"Sounds like all your other stories to me," he said at last.

"Well, it isn't," said William indignantly. "It's *abs'lutely* diff'rent. It's diff'rent from every other story I've ever written in all my life."

"You've had international gangs an' smugglers in nearly all of them," said Ginger. "There was the one where the man hid watches in jars of honey an' got stung to death by bees. Then there was the one where the man was head of an international gang that pretended to be frogmen an' had meetings in an ole wreck under the sea an' got caught by a seal that Scotland Yard had trained to catch international gangs that pretended to be frogmen an' had meetings in ole wrecks under——"

"But I tell you this is *diff'rent*," interrupted William impatiently.

"How's it diff'rent?" said Ginger, spitting out a mouthful of Worcester Pearmain. "There mus' be a *nest* of maggots about somewhere. Every single apple I try's full of 'em."

"Well, you can eat 'em, can't you?" said William. "They haven't any taste. I've eaten hundreds of 'em."

"Well, I'm not goin' to eat this one. It's nearly as big as a snake. Go on. Tell me how it's diff'rent."

"It's got real people in," said William.

"Gosh! Here's a wasp as well. Dunno whether it's after me or the apple or the maggot." He wobbled precariously on his branch. "It's gone now. I bet it didn't like the look of the maggot . . . What d'you mean, got real people in it?"

"Well, a friend of Robert's came to tea on Sunday an' he writes stories. He mus' be jolly good, too, 'cause once he nearly got one published. Anyway, he said that people in stories ought to be *real*. He said if they weren't real they were jus'—jus' soulless puppets, he said."

"What does that mean?" said Ginger.

"It means they're not nat'ral."

"Well—gosh! They aren't meant to be," said Ginger. "They're in *stories*, aren't they?"

"Yes, but this man said they'd got to be real, even in stories. He said they'd got to be alive. He said that it was called the School of Nature an' that all really good writers b'longed to it, so I'm goin' to b'long to it too an' put real people in mine, not jus' soulless puppets."

"Seems a bit dotty to me," said Ginger. "Anyway, how can you get real people in?"

"I'm puttin' in the people that live round here," said William. "We know they're alive all right 'cause we see 'em walkin' about every day."

"Who?"

"Oh . . . Mr. Monks."

"Gosh! You can't put him in," said Ginger. "Not the Vicar. He's high up in the church. He knows the Bishop."

"They're prob'ly both in it," said William darkly.

"Then there's Gen'ral Moult. He's alive all right. I'm goin' to put him in."

"I don't see how he can be a crim'nal," said Ginger. "He fought in the Boer War."

"I bet he only did it to put people off the scent," said William. "I bet he was a diamond smuggler all the time."

"Seems to me you're going to get in a bit of a muddle with it," said Ginger, thoughtfully contemplating his apple core and wondering whether to throw it at William or the greenhouse roof or a corpulent thrush day-dreaming on the lawn.

"No, I'm not," said William. "What this man meant was that you could have a 'maginary story, but you've got to have real people to put in it. Don't you *see*?"

"No," said Ginger, absent-mindedly eating his core, "but never mind. Go on with it. Who else are you goin' to have?"

"Well, I've got to have people that are members of the golf club here."

"Mr. Monks isn't. Neither is Gen'ral Moult."

"No, but the gang've got to have one or two that aren't. It'd look a bit fishy if they didn't."

"It's goin' to look a bit fishy anyway . . . Well, who're you goin' to have that belong to the club?"

"Mr. Wakely. . . ."

"Gosh! You can't have *him* for a crim'nal. He's head of the p'lice."

"Yes, that's his cunnin'," said William. "He got himself made head of the p'lice to put people off the scent . . . Then there's Dr. Bell. He b'longs to the club."

"Yes, an' he's a crim'nal all right," said Ginger bitterly. "He's a poisoner, too. Gosh, I can still taste that medicine he gave me when I was ill las' week. I nearly died of it."

"I bet he knew you only wanted to get out of arithmetic," said William unfeelingly. "You got well jolly quick after you'd tasted it. Anyway, he b'longs to the club an' so does Mr. Kirkham."

"But he's the Mayor of Hadley," said Ginger. "You can't have a mayor in a smugglin' gang."

"Huh!" snorted William. "I bet he killed the real mayor an' made himself up to look like him."

"They seem a pretty bad lot," said Ginger dispassionately.

"'Course they are," said William. "They're *crim'nals*, I tell you. Well, anyway, all the people in the golf club b'long to this gang."

"What happens when people try an' join that aren't crim'nals an' think it's jus' an ordin'ry golf club?"

"Not many do. My father hasn't joined 'cause he says it's a rotten course. He b'longs to the one in Hadley. I bet they *keep* it a rotten course so's people won't want to join."

"Yes, but some must," said Ginger. "What happens to them?"

"They kill 'em off," said William simply. "They kill 'em off like flies. Gosh! When you come to think of it, ole Mr. Gregson died las' week an' he'd jus' joined the club." His voice sank to a low sinister note. "I bet he was beginning to know too much."

"He died of pneumonia," said Ginger.

"I bet one of 'em slipped a pneumonia germ into his beer," said William.

"Who's the head of them?" said Ginger.

"No one knows who's the head of them," said

William. "It's kept a dead secret. They call him X. But axshully it's a woman."

"A woman?" said Ginger incredulously.

"Yes. It's a jolly good idea to have a woman 'cause none of them suspect it. They guess it's someone jolly high up, an' sometimes they think it's the bank manager an' sometimes they think it's the station master but they never think of it bein' Miss Golightly."

"Miss *Golightly*!" gasped Ginger as his mind went to Miss Golightly, the Headmistress of Rose Mount School, grim-faced, tight-lipped, with brisk staccato voice.

"I thought she was a good one to have," said William complacently. "She's the last one they'd think of an' she's a villain of the deepest dye."

"Yes, she's that all right," said Ginger. "She gave Frankie Dakers' sister a hundred lines for nothin' at all—well, jus' for lettin' off a quiet little firework in French class. But—gosh! you'd never think she was an international smuggler. You——" He stopped and shrugged helplessly. "I keep forgettin' they're only people in a story . . . You know, I still think it's goin' to get us into a muddle. I think you'd far better stick to the way you used to do them."

"Well, I'm not goin' to," said William. "I'm goin' to join this School of Nature an' have real people in the story, not jus' soulless puppets."

"Who else are you goin' to have in?"

"Mr. Westonbury. He's got the *look* of a crim'nal."

Ginger pictured the earnest, worried little face of Mr. Westonbury.

"He looks pretty innocent to me," he said.

"That's their cunnin'" said William. "They've got to look innocent to put people off the scent. They'd get caught if they didn't. Then I'm goin' to have Lieutenant-Colonel Pomeroy an' Colonel Hetherly."

"But they've got titles," protested Ginger.

"They haven't really," said William. "They only pretend they have to put people off their track . . . Anyway, it's a jolly excitin' story. I've written some of it down already. Come back to our house an' I'll show it you."

"What do they all *do* in it?" said Ginger.

William dropped with carefree agility from branch to branch of the apple tree till he reached the ground.

"I'll tell you on the way," he said.

"Where does the story start?" said Ginger, pausing to pick up a couple of conkers. He shelled them with a few deft movements and slipped them into his pocket. "I dunno why they grow 'em with all this green stuff outside 'em. You've only got to take it off."

"It's nature," explained William simply. "Well, the story starts in South Africa—that's where they find diamonds, you know—an' one of this gang goes over there an' fills the tyres of his car solid with diamonds. Then he drives it back an' takes it across the channel in a ferry disguised as a fishin' boat, then he drives it to this golf club here an' puts it in the garage. Then, in the dead of night, they take the diamonds out of the tyres an' put 'em into golf balls. Then the nex' day they pretend to play golf an' play with these balls an' keep losin' them in the long grass, but they know jus' where they are really an' next night someone goes round puttin' them into sacks an' fillin' up the tops of the sacks with potatoes, an' loads them on to lorries an' takes them up to Covent Garden and there's more of the gang at Covent

Garden disguised as greengrocers an' they take these sacks an' put them in their cars an' take 'em off to diamond fences."

"What's that?" said Ginger.

"Gosh, don't you know what a fence is? It's a person that buys stolen stuff an' a diamond fence is a person that buys smuggled diamonds. This gang makes *pounds* of money that way. They're *rollin'* in money. Why, look at Lieutenant-Colonel Pomeroy havin' that swimmin' pool made in his garden. My mother said it mus' have cost the earth. Well, that *proves* it, doesn't it?"

"Yes," agreed Ginger. "An' its a jolly good story. I think it's better even than the frogmen one."

They were passing the five-barred gate on which they were wont to practise their "vaulting." Automatically William stopped, hurled himself upon it and performed the ungainly semi-somersault that landed him head first on the other side.

"I never seem to get it quite right," he admitted as he picked himself up. "I think there's somethin' wrong with the gate."

"I think so, too," said Ginger when he had followed William's example with the same result. "Somethin' wrong with its balance. It sort of throws you over before you're ready."

They climbed on to the top rung and sat there side by side. William had picked up a stick blown down by a recent gale. He sat with his elbows on his knees, his frowning gaze bent on the ground, idly flicking the gate with his stick.

"Go on with the story," said Ginger. "What happens next?"

"Well, there's a man called Meredith at Scotland Yard an' one of the gang that's a traitor to them tips him off about this smugglin' gang an' he decides to come down here an' try an' unmask the plot. So he takes a cottage that's near the golf club an' pretends he's jus' come down for a golfin' holiday, but they find out who he is."

"I bet they finish him off pretty quick, then," said Ginger with gloomy relish.

"They'd like to," said William, "but they've got to find out who's betrayed them an' given him this tip first, so they invite him to the Golf Club Social—they have one every year, you know—an' they kidnap him an' put him to the most ghastly tortures to make him tell them who it was gave them away, but he won't. They're abs'lutely *ghastly* tortures. Miss Golightly thinks them up. She tells these crim'nals what to do by secret radio that no one knows where it comes from 'cause they still don't know who this X is. . . . Come on. Let's get on home now."

They jumped from the gate and went on down the road, William twirling his stick in airy nonchalant manner.

"Who're you goin' to have for this Meredith man?" said Ginger.

"I couldn't find anyone good enough for him," said William. "I thought 'em all over an' I couldn't find one that would make a decent hero."

"Well, no," agreed Ginger, holding a mental review of the inhabitants of the village. "There isn't anyone really heroic, is there? Robert *looks* all right, but——"

"Oh Robert!" said William scornfully. "He'd start

fallin' in love with all these crim'nals' daughters the minute he saw them. He'd never get round to doin' any detectin'."

"What are you goin' to do, then?"

"I'm makin' one up," said William.

"You're not goin' to have him real like the others?"

"No, but I've thought about him so much that he's real, all right. He's not jus' a soulless puppet."

"What's he like?"

"Gosh, he's fine," said William, his voice fired with sudden enthusiasm. "He's big an' strong an' brave. He's got red hair an' he's got a bit of a limp, too, with havin' all these narrow squeaks, snatchin' himself out of the jaws of death at Scotland Yard. An' he's so brave he's jus' not afraid of anythin'."

"He sounds all right," said Ginger judicially. "I hope he'll be a match for all these crim'nals."

"*'Course* he will," said William. "He——"

He stopped short. They were passing the gate of Clematis Cottage. A car had just drawn up at the gate. The door of the car opened and a young man got out. He was tall and muscular. He had red hair and, as he moved round the car to open the boot, they noticed that he walked with a slight limp.

William's mouth dropped open. His usually ruddy face had paled.

"Gosh!" he said beneath his breath. "Meredith!"

The young man turned to them with a pleasant smile.

"Hello," he said. "You live hereabouts?"

William nodded. The power of speech had deserted him.

"Well, perhaps you'd give me a hand with getting this stuff out," said the young man.

WILLIAM'S MOUTH DROPPED OPEN. HIS USUALLY RUDDY FACE HAD PALED.
"GOSH!" HE SAID BENEATH HIS BREATH. "MEREDITH!"

He handed two suit-cases to William and Ginger, slung a bag of golf clubs over his shoulder, took a key from his pocket and unlocked the door. They entered the sunny little hall of Clematis Cottage.

The power of speech was gradually returning to William.

"You—you stayin' here?" he said hoarsely.

"Yes," answered the young man. "I've taken the place for a fortnight. I'm going to have a golfing holiday here to blow the cobwebs out of my head."

"G-g-golfing?" gasped William.

"Yes. Bung the things down here and let's have a look round."

They followed him into the kitchen. William's face still wore a pale and stricken look.

"You're n-not goin' to join the golf club *here*, are you?" he stammered.

"Yes, that's the idea," said the young man. "It's nice and handy, you know. Only a few minutes' walk."

"But you m-mustn't," protested William. "You—you'll be runnin' into deadly danger."

"Oh, come," said the young man smiling. "I've been warned that it's a pretty mouldy course, but deadly danger's a bit thick. However, let's introduce ourselves. We don't know each other's names yet, do we? What's yours?"

"William," said William, "an' this is Ginger."

"And mine is——"

"We know yours," put in William. "It's Meredith."

The young man raised his eyebrows.

"Meredith?" he said. "What on earth makes you think my name's Meredith?"

"We *know* it is," said Ginger solemnly.

"Well, it isn't," said the young man with a smile. "It's Wansford. Hugh Wansford. Now let's inspect the commissariat. The good lady said she'd get in some food for me."

He opened the larder door and began to take out packages. "Sweet biscuits. I certainly don't want those . . . Catch! Dates! I don't want those either . . . Catch! Potato crisps. Nasty fiddly things! . . . Catch!"

"Thanks awfully," said William and Ginger, securing the packages.

"The rest seem all right—bacon, eggs, cheese." He opened the door of the frig. "Milk, chops, sausages. They should ward off starvation for a few days."

"You ought to keep your strength up," said William, sinking his voice to a low mysterious note, "for all you've got to go through."

"Yes, it'll be quite strenuous," said the young man. "I'm badly out of practice."

William bent a searching look on him and spoke with slow emphasis.

"You've come for somethin' else as well as golf, haven't you?" he said.

Again the young man laughed.

"If that's a shot in the dark, it's a lucky one," he said. "Well, actually, I have, but I'm not goin' to start on it till I've put in a few days' golf and general relaxation."

"Listen," said William. His face was tensed, his brows knit till they almost met over his earnest gaze. "Don't join this golf club here."

"Why ever not?"

"W—well," temporised William, "it's a rotten course for one thing. My father says it's a menace, an' he ought to know. He once won a prize for golf."

"Oh, I'm not all that choosy," said the young man. "I'm a rotten player anyhow. You'd better run off now, boys, and I'll try to get myself organised. Thanks for helping."

William and Ginger walked slowly down the road.

"He's jolly decent, isn't he?" said Ginger.

"'Course he is," said William. "I told you he was."

"Biscuits an' dates *an'* potato crisps! Let's go to the old barn an' eat them."

"All right," said William, "an' we've got to make our plans, too. We've got to plan how we can save him from this deadly danger he's goin' into. He doesn't know what he's up against. They stick at nothin', don't that gang."

A puzzled expression flitted over Ginger's face.

"But—his name's not Meredith," he said, clinging to this thin, frail thread of reality.

"Well, nat'rally he's got to pretend to be someone else when he's on a job like this," said William. "Detectives have got to have aliases same as crim'nals. They've got to try to put each other off the scent an' get each other into muddles."

They sat on the floor of the old barn and set to work on the biscuits.

"They're jolly good," said Ginger indistinctly.

"Yes, we've *got* to try 'n' help him after this," said William. "Look at this one. It's got sugar on the top an' chocolate inside. It's smashin'."

"An' these with pink cream in are smashin', too." said Ginger.

"An' so are these," said William. "The ones with blobs of jam in the middle." The earnest expression returned to his face. "It's goin' to be jolly diff'cult to help him 'cause we've got to pretend we don't know who he is. You see, Scotland Yard like workin' on their own. He'd try an' put us right off if he thought we knew. He wouldn't let us go anywhere near him, an' then we wouldn't be able to help him at all. We've got to be jolly careful . . . I say! Biscuits an' potato crisps taste jolly good together, don't they?"

"Yes," said Ginger," an' they taste better still mixed with dates. I'm goin' to try a sort of sandwich with a date in the middle an' a potato crisp an' a biscuit on each side."

They munched in silence for some time, then William said, "They've prob'ly found out by now that this Meredith's a high-up person from Scotland Yard an' that he's on their tracks."

"Y—yes," said Ginger. The faintly puzzled expression flickered over his face again, then vanished as he finally gave up all attempt to disentangle fact and fiction in his mind. In William's they now formed a glorious kaleidoscope, full of movement and colour and romance. "Yes, of course."

Mr. Wansford was mildly surprised to find himself closely shadowed by the two boys for the next few days. He dismissed them brusquely when he came upon them examining the contents of his golf bag and testing his clubs. (William suspected that a bomb might have been placed there by his enemies). They then turned their attention to the course itself and carried on a extensive examination of its equipment, paying special attention to the tee boxes, which William considered might be a convenient hiding place for the diamonds, until they were ejected by an indignant secretary who refused to accept—or even listen to—their carefully prepared excuse of "nature study".

But on the following day the annual fair arrived at Hadley and, in the excitement of visiting it—in authorised or unauthorised fashion—every day, they completely forgot Meredith and the desperate gang of criminals ranged against him. It was not till he saw an announcement of the Golf Club Social that William was recalled to a sense of his duty. Consternation and dismay swept over him.

"Gosh, Ginger," he said, "we can't let him go to that. That's where they kidnap him an' put him to all those ghastly tortures. I wish I hadn't made them so ghastly now. I wish I hadn't made them pull out his teeth *an'* his hair. We ought to've been doin' somethin' all this time. There he is, gettin' nearer an' nearer the jaws of death an' we've done nothin' at all."

"P'raps he won't go to this Social thing," said Ginger reassuringly.

"I bet they'll make him," said William. "I bet they'll *fetch* him if he doesn't. They've found out who he is an' what he's doin' an' they've got this kidnappin' an' torturin' all fixed up. Miss Golightly's *set* on it. She's determined to find out who gave the gang away . . . I shouldn't be s'prised if it was General Moult."

"Or Mr. Wakely," said Ginger. "He's head of the p'lice an' he might be playin' a double game."

"I wish I hadn't made those tortures so ghastly," said William. "There's one where they hang him up by his feet with his head in a bucket of water. I wish I hadn't put that one in."

"Could we go to the golf course again an' find some *proof* an' get 'em all put in prison before this Golf Social thing comes off?"

"Gosh, no! They're on the look-out for us. Why, they sent us off that time we jus' went to do a bit of quiet nature study. That showed they've got guilty consciences, all right."

"We did mess up the tee boxes, you know," Ginger reminded him.

"Huh! That was nothin'." said William. "They jus' used that to stop us findin' out their guilty secrets. *Tell* you what we mus' do . . . warn Meredith."

"When?"

"Now. Come on!"

They found Mr. Wansford in the kitchen of Clematis Cottage, clearing away the remains of his lunch.

"Hello!" he greeted them cheerfully. "How are you getting on?"

"All right, thanks," said William.

"Have a banana," said Mr. Wansford, pointing to a dish of fruit on the table.

"Thanks," said William, putting a banana in his pocket and handing one to Ginger. Then he cleared his throat portentously and added, "You goin' to this Golf Club Social?"

"Yes," said Mr. Wansford. "One might as well be sociable. Have a pear."

"Thanks," said William, selecting the two largest. "I say . . ."

"Yes?"

"I—I don't think you ought to go to that Social."

Mr. Wansford looked at him in surprise.

"Why ever not?"

"There's reasons," said William darkly.

"The jaws of death," said Ginger.

"Fiends in human shape," said William.

"Oh, come!" laughed Mr. Wansford. "You've been listening to one of the more disgruntled members. Some of them do play a pretty selfish game, I admit, but—

fiends in human shape! Definitely not! Now run off, boys. I have a lot to do this afternoon."

Reluctantly they left the cottage and made their way down the road to William's house.

"He's set on goin'," said William gloomily, peeling his banana and throwing the skin into the ditch, "an' he's tryin' to put us off the scent."

"Seems like it," agreed Ginger.

"I think he's beginnin' to suspect we know too much," said William. "How many bites can you eat your banana in?"

A silent contest took place.

"I did mine in four," said Ginger at last.

"I did mine in three," said William. "I won. Well, now, listen . . . We've *got* to stop him goin' to that Social thing. There's one torture where they put nettles in his shoes an' make him walk about in them. I wish I hadn't thought of that one. It's ghastly. Well, we've got to do somethin'."

"What?" said Ginger.

"Oh, shut up!" said William. "Give me a bit of peace to think in, can't you."

Ginger turned his eyes hopefully and respectfully on his friend and kept silence till William suddenly stopped short. The cloud had lifted from his brow. It shone with the light of a dawning idea.

"I think I've got it," he said. "Now listen. This Social thing's tomorrow night an' we've got to stop him goin' to the Club for it, 'cause if he did he'd get kidnapped an' tortured, so we'll have to find somewhere else for him to go to so that he'll *think* he's goin' to the Social but isn't really."

"Y—yes?" said Ginger with mingled doubt and apprehension in his voice. "But where?"

"Well, there's The Hall," said William.

"The Hall? I don't see how that comes into it."

"Gosh, aren't you stupid!" said William helplessly. "It's empty, isn't it? The Botts are away."

"Yes, but there's a caretaker there."

"Ole Mr. Miggs. . . . Yes, but it's Thursday tomorrow an' on Thursdays he goes over to Marleigh to see his daughter an' then he calls at all the pubs on his way home an' doesn't get back till late. I've heard people talkin' about it."

"Well?" said Ginger.

"Well, don't you *see*! We can get this Mr. Meredith to go to The Hall 'stead of the Club an' we can keep him there till the danger's over."

"How can we?" said Ginger.

"We'll have the front door open. I can open it 'cause I know where Mrs. Bott keeps her spare key in the tool-shed, an' when he's gone in we'll put Jumble to guard the front door. He ought to be able to do it all right. He's had enough p'lice dog trainin'."

"He's never really taken to it," put in Ginger.

William ignored the interruption.

"An' we'll fix up somethin' at the back door so's he can't get out."

"But how're you goin' to get him in, to start with?"

"Oh, it'll be easy enough," said William airily. "I'll jus' send him a message."

"I bet it won't be as easy as *that*!" said Ginger.

But, oddly enough, it was.

An ancient crone called Mrs. Parkinson came for an hour each morning to "do" Clematis Cottage. During that hour she mooched about the cottage with mop and feather duster, idly flicking such objects as came within her range of vision. It was while she was engaged in flicking her feather duster over the surface of the kitchen linoleum that the telephone bell rang. A deep gruff voice informed her that it wished to leave a message for Mr. Meredith, correcting the name almost immediately afterwards to Mr. Wansford. Mrs. Parkinson fetched a pencil and wrote down the message on the paper the bread had been wrapped in, hung it on the hatstand, and returned to her feather dusting.

William and Ginger, with Jumble in unwilling attendance, lurked near the gate of Clematis Cottage the next evening to watch Mr. Wansford emerge from his front door, then followed him down the road with mounting anxiety till he reached the lane that led to the golf club. He passed it and continued his way down the road that led to The Hall.

"Good!" said William with a sigh of relief. "We've saved him! Gosh! Think of 'em all there waitin' for him with all those ghastly tortures an' him not turnin' up. I 'spect they're all there 'cept Miss Golightly. She'll be at Rose Mount sending out secret radio messages that they don't know where they come from telling them when to start the tortures an' how long to do them an' that sort of thing."

"P'raps he's not goin' to The Hall," said Ginger. "P'raps he's jus' goin' into the village to get some cigarettes . . ."

"No, he's not," said William. "*Look!* He's goin' into The Hall gates."

And, sure enough, Mr. Wansford was turning into the

gateway of The Hall and making his way slowly and rather uncertainly up the drive.

William and Ginger had not been idle during the day. Besides the telephone call (for which William had practised his "grown-up" voice till he was almost too hoarse to speak) they had secured the spare key to the front door, unlocked it and left it ajar.

Jumble had been enlisted in their service under protest. Jumble disliked his police-dog role and evaded it whenever possible. He had evolved a technique of non-co-operation that he was finding highly successful: he simply behaved as if he were not there at all. He allowed himself to be led—or dragged—to the scene of his police duties and there he lay down and dozed till his term of duty was over. He accompanied William and Ginger now in the aimless fashion of a sleep-walker as they followed Mr. Wansford up the drive of The Hall, slipping from the cover of one shrub to the cover of the next, concealing themselves hastily whenever he seemed about to turn round.

Mr. Wansford hesitated for a moment at the front door, rang the bell, waited, rang the bell again, hesitated again for a few more moments, then pushed open the door and vanished inside.

"Got him!" said William triumphantly. "Let's fix Jumble an' then go round to the back."

Jumble, assigned his post on the front door mat, stretched himself out as comfortably as he could, his nose between his paws.

"On guard! Good dog!" whispered William.

Jumble opened one eye, gave William a sardonic glance and settled down to sleep.

William and Ginger went round to the back of the

THEY FOLLOWED MR. WANSFORD UP THE DRIVE OF THE HALL, SLIPPING FROM THE COVER OF ONE SHRUB TO THE COVER OF THE NEXT.

house, fixed up a wire entanglement at the back door which, they thought, would effectively prevent their prisoner's escape, then crept round to the long veranda that sheltered the library window and peered cautiously through the glass.

The library was a square, little-used room. The Botts' tastes were not literary and the books that lined the walls had a decorative rather than functional purpose. The room had two doors. One, made of oak, led into the hall. The other, inadequately camouflaged by painted books (a "whim" of Mrs. Bott's), led into a small breakfast room beyond.

Mr. Wansford was there, walking to and fro, glancing every now and then at his watch, gazing about him with a slightly bewildered expression. Occasionally he would stop by the bookshelves, take down a book, turn over a page or two, put it back and continue his restless pacing to and fro.

"I wish he could find an excitin' book," whispered William. "Then he'd get int'rested an' forget the time an'——"

He stopped. The colour had faded from his cheeks.

"Gosh," he breathed.

For the camouflaged door was slowly opening.

It opened to its full and——

Miss Golightly appeared in the aperture.

"Gosh!" said William again. "We've led him straight into the jaws of death."

"How did she know he was here?" whispered Ginger.

"I dunno, but she did," said William. "Be quiet an' let's try an' hear what they're sayin'."

The two inside the room were speaking to each other, but William and Ginger could hear no words. They could only see the movements of their lips.

"I bet she's sayin' that if he doesn't tell her who gave the gang away she'll start puttin' him to those tortures. . . . He's talkin' now. He's tellin' her he won't . . ."

"She's talkin' now," said Ginger.

"Yes, she's tellin' him that she's got the tortures all ready in the dungeon——"

"There isn't one."

"There's a coal cellar that can be used as a dungeon. I bet she's got 'em all ready. He's talkin' now. He's tellin' her that his lips are sealed."

"She's talkin' now. I bet she's tellin' him about hangin' him up by his feet with his head in a bucket of water . . ."

"Come on!" said William. "We've got to rescue him."

"How can we?"

"I tell you, we've *got* to. I once read about some people rescuin' a person by creatin' a disturbance an' shoutin' 'Fire!' an' then rescuin' the person while the disturbance was goin' on. An'—*tell* you what! We can do more than that. There's a real fire extinguisher we can squirt at her. I know where it's kept 'cause I watched Mr. Bott fillin' it up an' puttin' it away in the hall. He put water in it 'cause he said he hadn't any of the right stuff an' anyway water made less of a mess than the right stuff, an' I bet if we squirted water out of it at Miss Golightly we'd get her so's she couldn't see or hear an' then while she couldn't see or hear we'd rescue Meredith."

"Yes, but how?" said Ginger. "I bet she'll turn savage when we've got her at bay. I bet she's got the strength of ten when she's at bay. A villainess iike that would have."

"Tell you what!" said William. "We'll corner her."

"Corner her?"

"Yes. There's a sort of trolley in the hall an' one of

us can shoot the water out at her an' the other can run the trolley at her an' pin her in a corner of the room so she can't escape an'—an' rescue Meredith. . . . Come on. Let's get started." He paused for a moment or two to watch the couple inside the room. "They're talkin'. He's shakin' his head . . . He's still sayin' he won't . . . Come on quick!"

Mr. Wansford had turned sharply from the bookshelves when Miss Golightly entered the room.

"Oh . . ." she said. "I don't know who you are, but the Botts are away."

"The Botts?" he said vaguely.

"Yes. They've shut up the house and gone to Scotland for a month or two. My name's Miss Golightly. I'm having rather large-scale alterations done at my school, and Mrs. Bott kindly said I could spend a night here whenever the invasion became too much for me. It's become too much for me today so I've taken refuge here."

"But—I understood that the Golf Club Social was being held here."

Miss Golightly stared at him.

"However did you get that idea?" she said.

"Mrs. Parkinson gave me the message. She wrote it down but she may have got it confused."

"Knowing Mrs. Parkinson," said Miss Golightly dryly, "I should think it more than likely. I haven't met you before, by the way, have I?"

"My name's Wansford. I've come here for a short golfing holiday and I've joined the club as a temporary member."

"How odd!" said miss Golightly. "I mean I can't

THE TWO DOORS BURST OPEN. WILLIAM CHARGED THROUGH
CHARGED THROUGH THE OTHER,

quite understand why anyone should choose this particular neighbourhood for a golfing holiday. I don't play the game myself, but I'm told the course is infamous."

"It's not too good," said Mr. Wansford, "but actually I had another object in coming here. I have an aunt who's fanatically interested in the family history, as aunts are apt to be, and she persuaded me to come along to this district to find out what I can about a branch of the family that used to live around here. They migrated to Australia in 1840, and my aunt is most anxious to find out whether any trace of them can be found."

"What was the name of the man who emigrated?"

"Thomas Golightly."

"Oh, but how thrilling! I'm a native of these parts

ONE, BRANDISHING HIS FIRE EXTINGUISHER, AND GINGER HURTLING HIS TROLLEY BEFORE HIM.

myself, you know, and Thomas Golightly was my great grandfather. His grandson, my father, returned here, but he was completely uninterested in the family. Now I, on the contrary, have always been intensely interested and I've always meant, when I had more leisure, to try to discover the other branches of the family."

"I must put you in touch with my aunt," said Mr. Wansford. "She has a whole roomful of papers and diaries and family trees. She'll be delighted to hear that I've found the missing branch."

"And I'm delighted to find the missing tree," said Miss Golightly. "Now do tell me——" She stopped and looked round. "I thought I heard the sound of scuffling outside in the hall. I——"

And then the two doors burst open.

William charged through one, brandishing his fire extinguisher, and Ginger charged through the other, hurtling his trolley before him. But, unfortunately, no rehearsal had been possible and their sense of direction misfired. They charged across the room full tilt into each other. William directed his fire extinguisher into Ginger's face and Ginger drove his trolley with all his might against William's solid form. The two struggled on the floor amid the wreckage of the trolley.

"Fire!" shouted William

"Murder!" shouted Ginger.

"Help!" shouted Mr. Miggs, returning from his outing and falling into the wire-netting entanglement.

The wreckage of the trolley had been cleared away, and William and Ginger were gradually recovering their breath.

Miss Golightly was addressing them in her best headmistress manner.

Mr. Wansford watched in ever deepening bewilderment.

"I know, of course, that it's an empty house, for the time being," said Miss Golightly, "but that's no reason why you boys should appropriate it as a playground."

"Yes, but——" panted William.

"You have no consideration whatever for other people's property," said Miss Golightly. "It's outrageous! That you should have the impertinence to come *here* in the absence of the owners and use the house for playing trains or Cowboys and Indians or whatever idiotic game you were playing!"

"Listen——" began William, but the flood of Miss Golightly's eloquence swept over him unabated.

"You are too old in any case to be playing those rough, senseless, childish games. You deserve to be taught a sharp lesson and if this were not a very important day in my life—a day in which you might say I have found a long-lost relative—I should see that you received it."

William turned to Mr. Wansford.

"Aren't you—aren't you a detective?" he said.

"A detective?" said Miss Golightly.

"Good Lord, no!" said Mr. Wansford. "What on earth are you talking about?"

"Nothin'," said William, emerging shattered and bewildered into the world of reality. "Nothin'."

"The trolley can no doubt be easily repaired," said Miss Golightly, "so we will say no more about the matter except that if ever you set foot here again without permission you will be most severely dealt with . . . Now off you go!"

William and Ginger turned towards the door. Miss Golightly and Mr. Wansford continued their conversation.

"My aunt has some very interesting diaries," said Mr. Wansford, "that give fascinating details about the family. For instance there was a Cavalier who spent two days and two nights on the roof while Roundheads ransacked his house searching for him. His family sent food up to him through a trap-door and——"

"One moment!" said Miss Golightly. She turned a freezing eye upon William and Ginger, who still hovered in the doorway. "Go away at *once*, you two!"

William and Ginger went out of the room, out of the front door and down the drive to the gate.

Jumble, who had left his post and was lurking in the shelter of a laurel bush, joined them at the gate and sloped along behind them. His tail was down. He looked sheepish and guilty, well aware that he had once more failed to fulfil his role. He was not repentant, merely abashed. The three trailed disconsolately down the road.

"Well, I bet you won't write any more stories," said Ginger at last, bitterly.

"Oh, I dunno," said William. Something of his old aplomb was returning, the ghost of his old swagger was invading his walk. "That Cavalier on the roof'd make a jolly good tale. I could have Roundheads chasing him all over it an' up an' down the chimneys. I could make it jolly excitin'."

"But you won't put real people into it, will you?" said Ginger anxiously.

"No, I jolly well won't," said William. "I'm not goin' to have anythin' more to do with that School of Nature. I'm goin' back to soulless puppets."

III

WILLIAM'S ESCAPE ROUTE

"MY father's got a book out of the library about war-time escapes," said Henry. "I've been readin' it an' it's jolly int'restin'."

"Yes, I know," said Ginger. "Tunnels."

"Wooden horses," said Douglas.

"Disguises," said William.

William, Ginger, Henry and Douglas were sitting huddled together in William's tent in the Browns' garden. It was a dilapidated tent of ancient design with a disconcerting habit of collapsing on its inmates suddenly and for no apparent cause. Every summer they would drag it out from the recesses of the garden shed, devote much time and energy to setting it up and play their parts in it as explorers, Red Indians, Eskimos, road-menders or mountaineers till it collapsed and had to be set up again. This morning they had been first Eskimos and then Red Indians, and the tent had collapsed on them with monotonous regularity whenever their roles reached a certain pitch of excitement.

"It jus' won't let us *get* anywhere," grumbled Ginger. "It came down jus' when you were wrestlin' with that polar bear an' jus' when I was goin' to scalp Henry."

"I bet you couldn't have scalped me," said Henry. "I bet you couldn't scalp anyone if you tried. I bet it's jolly difficult. It mus' take years of practice."

"It'd be easy enough scalpin' anyone with hair," said Douglas, "but bald ones would be difficult. I expect they have to have special trainin' for doin' bald ones."

"If I was an Indian I'd tattoo the bald ones," said William. "I can't think why bald people don't get their heads tattooed, anyway. It'd make them look a lot more int'restin' an'——"

At this point the tent collapsed again, engulfing them in folds of threadbare canvas.

"It's a rotten tent," said Douglas as he crawled out. "We'll get suffocated in it one of these days."

"Well, a bit of wind must have come," said William, rising as usual to a half-hearted defence of his tent. "Gosh! Any tent's li'ble to come down in a gale."

"Well, what'll we do now?" said Ginger.

"Let's go 'n' eat windfalls in the apple tree," said William.

They went to the bottom of the garden and climbed up the gnarled old apple tree that afforded a comfortable seat for each of them in its thick curving lichen-covered branches. William had given a liberal interpretation to his mother's injunction, "only eat the windfalls".

"You see," he said, "if they come off at a little touch it means they'd have come off in the wind, so they're windfalls."

"An' if they come off at a big touch," said Ginger, "it means they'd come off in a strong wind, so they're still windfalls."

"I bet there's not all *that* wind," said Henry with a touch of disapproval in his voice as he watched William's efforts to secure a large red apple that grew just above his head.

"It blew the tent down," William reminded him as he secured the apple and drove his teeth into it.

They munched in comparative silence for some minutes, then the process ended, as it generally did, in a competition of core-throwing, and it was not till a core, thrown by William and aimed at the drain-pipe, sailed through the open kitchen window to land in the middle of a half-made shepherd's pie, that the four found themselves summarily ejected from the premises and making their way down the road in the direction of the village.

"It was a jolly good shot, axshully," said William. "Right in the middle of that pie."

"But you weren't aiming at the pie," said Henry.

William knit his brows.

"I'm not sure I wasn't," he said.

"You said the drain-pipe."

"I might have changed my mind."

"You didn't."

"I did."

"You didn't."

They stopped in the middle of the road and a short, sharp wrestling match took place, at the end of which they picked themselves up and continued amicably on their way.

"What were we talkin' about?"

"Pies."

"No, before that."

"Scalpin' bald people."

"No, before that."

"About that book Henry had been readin'."

"Yes," said Henry. "It was about prisoners escapin' from war prisons. Gosh! Some of them were smashin' escapes."

"Yes, I've heard of 'em," said William, "an' I bet I could escape from a war prison jus' as well as any of 'em."

"I bet you couldn't."

"I bet I could . . . I've got out of places that no one'd ever have thought I could get out of. I once got out of a shed that——"

"Well, I bet you couldn't get out of a *prison*. A prison's a bit diff'rent from a shed an'——"

"I bet I *could*."

"I'd like to see you try."

"All right. See me try. Lock me up in a prison an' *see* if I can't get out."

"We can't shut you up in a prison 'cause we haven't got one."

"Well, then, you can't say I couldn't get out 'cause you don't know an' I bet I *could*. You can't *prove* I couldn't, anyway."

"An' you can't prove you *could*, 'cause we've not got a prison. Well, there isn't a prison anywhere round here an' if there was they wouldn't lend it us jus' to see if you could get out of it."

A thoughtful look had come into Henry's face.

"Wait a minute," he said. "There's Meadowview . . ."

"Meadowview . . ." said William. "It's a jolly funny name for a prison an' I bet they won't lend it you."

"It's not a prison," said Henry. "It's one of those houses in Green Lane. An old man called Mr. Fellowes used to live there an' he died las' month an' left this house to his nephew 'cause this nephew's the executor an'——"

"What are you *talkin'* about?" broke in William

irritably. "I'm tryin' to talk about prisoners escapin' from prison an' you start talkin' about dead old men an' executioners. It doesn't make sense."

"No, but *listen,*" said Henry. "Jus' wait till I've finished. This old man had a housekeeper called Miss Barrows——"

"Yes, my mother knows her," put in Ginger.

"An' this housekeeper's stayin' on in this house jus' till this nephew——"

"The executioner?" said William.

"Well, yes . . . jus' till he's got time to see to things an' sell the house, an' she's gone away on a holiday now an' left the key with my mother 'cause the police always want to know who you've left the key with when you go away an'—well, it jolly well *is* a prison. All the windows are fastened by burglar catches an' this housekeeper's taken all the keys away with her an' the back door's fastened by a special burglar lock an' she's taken the key of that away, too. An' the front door has a funny sort of lock that if you give it a double turn locks it so's you can't even open it from inside an'——'

"Yes?" said William.

"Well, don't you *see*?" said Henry. "I could get this key from my mother. I mean, I know where she keeps it an' she's goin' to London all day tomorrow so I could get it easy."

"Gosh, yes, I see," said William. "It's a jolly good idea. You an' Douglas can lock me an' Ginger in this house an' we'll do a war escape out of it, won't we Ginger?"

"Yes, I bet we will," said Ginger, infected as usual, despite his better judgement, by William's enthusiasm.

"'*Course* we will," said William. "When'll we start?"

"Well, my mother's goin' up to London by the nine thirty-one," said Henry, "so I can get the key any time after that."

"All right," said William. "We'll meet at this house at half past nine."

"Yes," agreed Henry, "an' we'll lock you into it an' give you till lunch time to get out."

"Huh!" snorted William. "I bet we won't need all *that* time. I bet we'll be out in ten minutes."

"All right," said Henry. "Half past nine tomorrow."

At half past nine the four met outside Meadowview. It was a Georgian house set well back from the road, with two rows of sash windows and a small pillared porch, approached by a semi-circular drive with two wooden gates. They stood for some moments casting furtive glances up and down the road. No one was in sight. Cautiously, in single file, they made their way up the short drive and mounted the four stone steps that led to the front door. Henry took the key from his pocket, inserted it in the keyhole and flung the door open. It revealed a fair-sized hall with polished chest, wardrobe and a hat rack composed of spreading antlers.

They entered and stood considering their surroundings with critical interest.

"I bet I could do somethin' with those stag horns," said William. "If I could find a fur rug I might go out disguised as a stag."

"Yes, an' how are you goin' to *get* out?" said Henry.

"There's nothin' to stop a prisoner of war breakin' a window," said William. "He could do it when no one was lookin'."

"You couldn't break those windows," said Douglas. "They're all divided into tiny little panes by wood."

"Small-paned sash windows," said Henry. "Georgian."

"Well, I can't stay chatterin' to you all day, wastin' my escape time," said William with dignity. "You'd better go now."

"All right," said Henry. "We'll come an' let you out at lunch time."

The door slammed behind him. William and Ginger heard the sound of the key being turned in the lock and footsteps going down the drive.

"Well, come on," said William. "Let's start." He pushed open one of the doors that led off from the hall. "Here's the dinin' room. I'm gettin' hungry, aren't you? Let's see if there's anything to eat." He knelt down, opened a sideboard cupboard, and inserted head and shoulders into it. "Nothin' at all," he announced disapprovingly as he emerged. "A biscuit tin with nothin' in it an' a date box with jus' two date stones in it. Gosh! They *might* have left jus' a few biscuits an' a date or two."

"They didn't know we were comin'," said Ginger mildly. "Anyway, we're s'posed to be escapin' not eatin'."

"Yes, I know," said William, "but there's no reason why we shouldn't do a bit of both."

He returned to the hall. Though he had not lost sight of the main object of his enterprise, he could not resist the temptation to investigate any interesting side-lines that offered themselves.

"I bet this is the sitting-room," he said, opening another door. "Yes, it is. There's a nice big chimney

THERE CAME A RATTLE AND A CLATTER AND WILLIAM DESCENDED IN A SHOWER OF BRICKWORK AND SOOT.

here. I bet we could get out that way. I'll have a look." He knelt down on the hearth-rug and again his head and shoulders disappeared from view. His voice came muffled from the chimney aperture. "Yes, I bet I could climb up this an' get out on to the roof an' down by a drain-pipe." More of his person vanished from view and his voice seemed to come from a farther distance. "If I could get hold of somethin' to pull myself up by. . . There's nothin' to hold. Wait a minute. Yes, there is. Yes, I've got hold of somethin'." His legs—all that could now be seen of him—waved wildly in the air. "Yes, I can . . . No, I can't." There came a rattle and a clatter and he descended in a shower of brickwork and soot. "No, there's nothin' to get hold of," he complained as he scrambled to his feet, "an' I bet they've not had it cleaned for years."

"Gosh, you have got in a mess," said Ginger.

"Well, I bet real escapers get in worse ones," said William philosophically. "Anyway, it all helps to make a disguise 'case I need one." He turned to inspect the window. "We can't get out that way. They're locked an' if you broke one you couldn't even get your head out. Let's have a look at the other rooms."

He crossed the hall and opened another door.

"Here's the kitchen . . . an' I bet this is the larder. Let's have a look at the larder."

The larder provided a depressing spectacle of empty shelves except in one corner, where a small jar of honey appeared to have been overlooked.

"Come on," said William, unscrewing the lid. "Gosh! It's only quarter full. They're the meanest set of people in this house I ever came across. Anyway, let's find somethin' to eat it with." He opened a drawer in the kitchen table and inspected the contents. "Fish slice, corkscrew, screwdriver . . . I 'spect we can manage with the screwdriver. We'll have it in turns. I'll start." He rammed the tool into the jar and brought out a blob of honey.

"Your turn," he said, handing screwdriver and jar to Ginger.

"A lot's gone on your face," said Ginger. "It's got mixed up with the soot."

"It'll help clean it up," said William. "Gosh, they might have left a bit more honey . . . I'm goin' to have another look in the larder. There's a cake tin there an' it might have a bit of cake in it."

"We're s'posed to be gettin' out of this house," Ginger reminded him again, "not settlin' down in it."

"Well, you've got to get to *know* a place before you can escape from it," said William. "I'm workin' all the time. I'm gettin' to know the background so's I can plan the escape prop'ly. An' anyway we've got to eat to keep our strength up, haven't we? We've no idea what life-an'-death dangers we'll have to go through before we get out, an' we want to get out alive, don't we? So we've got to keep our strength up. . . . Here's a couple of carrots left in the vegetable rack. They're not very big but they're nearly clean . . . Jus' *like* 'em not to leave more than two!"

Having disposed of his carrot in three and a half gigantic bites William turned his attention to the rest of the kitchen. A long-handled ceiling brush caught his attention.

"It'd make a jolly useful sort of tool," he said, brandishing it experimentally and sending a Family Butcher's calendar, which depicted a group of morose-looking Highland cattle, flying off its hook across the room. "Look! What's that thing with bars up in the wall?"

"A ventilator," said Ginger.

"I bet we could escape through that. We could knock it out an' it would leave a hole an' we could sort of—enlarge the hole an' escape. I bet I could reach it with this brush thing. Look! I'll get on this chair an' I'll jab the end of this brush thing into the ventilator an' push it out. . . ."

He mounted a chair and thrust his ceiling brush in the direction of the ventilator—thrust it with such force that he lost his balance, slipped from his chair and fell headlong. The brush swept the chimney shelf in its descent, sending several blue and white jars crashing to the ground and scattering their contents—rice, sugar, currants and candied peel—in all directions.

"Gosh!" said William, looking at them in dismay, "I didn't mean to do that. . . . It was a jolly good idea but the handle wasn't quite long enough. If it'd been a bit longer I'd have pushed it open an' then we'd have enlarged the hole an' we'd have been out by now. We'd have got on the roof an' slid down a drain-pipe."

"Well, we haven't done," said Ginger, "so we'll have to think of somethin' else."

"I bet I can think of somethin' else all right," said William. "Let's try upstairs. There's often int'restin' things in a bathroom."

There were several interesting things in the bathroom, among them a spray, to which William turned his whole attention, giving liberal sprinklings of it to himself, Ginger and the floor.

"I wish you'd remember that we're s'posed to be gettin' *out*," said Ginger.

"Well, we've got to do a bit of experimentin' to find *how* to get out, haven't we?" said William. "I bet real prisoners used water sprays to get out. There mus' be some way of usin' a water spray to get out. If there was a guard underneath the window we could stun him by a sudden burst of water an' get out before he came to."

"Well, there isn't a guard underneath the window," said Ginger, "so we can't stun him. An' we couldn't open the window anyway, 'cause it's locked same as all the others. Come on. Let's try somethin' else."

"All right," said William, turning off the spray reluctantly. "Let's go an' see if there's anythin' interestin' in the bedrooms. I bet there won't be."

The bedrooms proved as devoid of interest as William had anticipated. He investigated wardrobes, cupboards, drawers and finally a square of three-ply wood behind an electric fire.

"I bet there's a chimney behind that," he said. "If I could get this piece of wood out, I could climb up it an' it'd be easier than the downstairs one 'cause it's nearer the roof."

"Well, you can't get that piece of wood out," said Ginger.

"I can have a try," said William.

He wrestled unsuccessfully for a few minutes, broke a nail, fell over backwards, then finally gave up the struggle.

"I don't think there *is* a chimney there." He tapped the wood and listened thoughtfully. "Sounds to me more like one of those secret rooms where clergymen used to hide up in the olden days."

"When did they?" said Ginger.

"Bronze Age or Stone Age or some time," said William vaguely.

"You're thinkin' of Druids," said Ginger.

"Maybe I am," said William, "but I know they used to hide up in secret rooms 'cause I once read a story about it."

"Well, let's get on with this escape," said Ginger impatiently.

William rose to his feet and looked round the room.

"All right," he said. "Let's try this tunnel idea. A lot of them got out by tunnels, so I don't see why we shouldn't."

"Well, we can't start a tunnel in a bedroom," said Ginger. "We've got to get down to a ground floor."

"There might be a cellar," said William. "We could make a tunnel easy in a cellar, 'cause it's half-way down in the earth to start with."

"We haven't any spades," objected Ginger.

"Well, we can find things that'll *do* for spades, can't we?" said William. "Let's go downstairs an' have a look."

They went downstairs and had a look. Under the staircase there was a small door that they had not noticed before. William opened it and peered down a dim, steep flight of steps.

"Gosh! It *is* a cellar," he said excitedly. "Come on! Let's find some tools an' go down an' start that tunnel. There was a poker an' a shovel in the sitting-room an' there was that fish slice an' corkscrew an' screwdriver thing in the kitchen drawer."

Ginger fetched poker and shovel, William armed himself with fish slice, corkscrew, and screwdriver, and the two began the descent. The steps led down into a large, dark, earth-smelling room with a floor of brickwork and roughly whitewashed walls, festooned by cobwebs. The place was dark and airless. A small barred window, set high up in the wall and covered by dust, admitted a faint blurred light.

"I BET NO ONE'S BEEN HERE FOR HUNDREDS OF YEARS," SAID GINGER.

"I bet no one's been here for hundreds of years," said Ginger.

William was inspecting the brick floor.

"I wonder where's the best place to start the tunnel," he said.

"You can't dig through bricks," said Ginger.

"No, you idiot!" said William, "but you can take

up the bricks an' dig under them, can't you? There's *earth* under them, isn't there?"

"I bet they're stuck down jolly fast," said Ginger.

"They mus' be looser in some places than others," said William.

He began to examine the uneven floor, pausing every now and then to give experimental prods with fish slice or corkscrew. Then he stopped suddenly and stood scowling down at a patch of brickwork.

"They seem a bit loose here," he said. He gave the place another prod. "Yes, I bet I could move one or two of these an' it'd give me room to start the tunnel."

Dropping on to his knees, he began to prise the edge of the fish slice between the bricks while Ginger set to work with shovel and poker near the opposite wall.

They worked silently for a few minutes, then William gave a grunt.

"It's comin'," he said. "I'll try the corkscrew now. I'll try 'em both together. Where's the screwdriver . . .? It's comin'."

There was a rending and a grating sound. He gave a yell of triumph. "It's *come*! I *said* we'd do it, didn't I? I *said* we'd get out. Huh! Fancy them thinkin' we couldn't."

"We've not got out yet," said Ginger.

"We've as good as got out," said William. "We've started. We've got down to the *earth*. All we've got to do now is to dig the tunnel."

Ginger had left his own uncompleted work (he had only succeeded in scraping off a few layers of dirt and coal dust) and had come over to inspect William's.

"It won't be much of a tunnel," he said, "if it's only

goin' to be the size of a brick. Gosh! A *worm* couldn't escape through it."

"Don't be such a chump. I'm goin' to make it larger. I'm goin' to take another brick out. I've *got* it out. An' —look! There's somethin' underneath it."

Ginger crouched down to examine a smallish envelope, made of mackintosh, that had been revealed by the dislodging of the brick.

"What is it?" he said.

"Dunno," said William, "but I bet it's treasure of some sort. Pound notes or foreign stamps or coupons to send up for somethin'." He opened the envelope and drew out a yellow piece of paper. His expression changed to one of disgust. "Gosh! Jus' an' old bit of paper with some bits of music scribbled on it. I 'spect the man that made this floor was goin' on to his music lesson an' he dropped this music under this brick by accident an' never knew what had happened to it." He threw the envelope carelessly on one side and thrust the paper into his pocket. "Might come in useful. Bits of paper sometimes do. We might get in a muddle in this tunnel an' need some bits of paper to show us the way out. A man in a Greek story did that gettin' away from a bull."

Ginger had wandered over to the darkest corner of the cellar.

"I say! Come and look at this!" he called.

William laid down the fish slice and joined him.

A shelf of new wood supported a row of stone jars. A leaflet lay beside them entitled, "How to Make Ginger Beer."

"I remember Miss Barrows tellin' my mother she was goin' to try makin' that stuff," said Ginger. "This mus' be it. She said it went on makin' itself once you'd started it."

"Well, if it does that," said William, "it won't do any harm jus' to drink a bit of it. Do it good, 'cause it'd make more room for the new lot. I'm jolly thirsty, aren't you?"

"Yes," said Ginger.

"Well, come on. Let's have a drink."

"The corks look jolly tight."

"We can push 'em up a bit. I bet the fish slice'll do it. I'll try the fish slice an' the corkscrew *an'* the screw-driver. They ought to get it off between them."

He probed and prised for a few minutes then gave another yell of triumph.

"It's comin'," he said.

It came.

With a loud report the cork flew up to the ceiling while cascades of froth poured down the side of the bottle.

"Well, there's not goin' to be much left of that one," said William. "It's all comin' out in soap suds. Let's try another."

They tried another. The same thing happened. With a still louder report the cork flew up to the ceiling and a cascade of froth poured down the side of the jar.

"I'll try another," said William doggedly.

"Wait a minute," said Ginger. There was a warning note in his voice. "I think I can hear somethin'. Listen!"

Footsteps were coming along the drive. The dusty window revealed—faintly but unmistakably—a pair of stalwart boots advancing towards the front door.

"Who is it?" whispered Ginger.

"Dunno," said William. "It can't be Henry or Douglas. They've not got that sort of feet. Let's wait an' see."

Two loud knocks resounded through the house.

"P'raps it's jus' someone askin' the way somewhere or bringin' the Parish Magazine," said Ginger. "They'll go away soon."

They watched the window hopefully, but the feet did not reappear.

Two more knocks resounded through the house. Then suddenly there came a sound of an engine, and a small red car was seen passing the window and drawing up at the front door. They heard the sound of voices.

"They're talkin' to each other," said William. "I'm goin' up to see what's happenin'."

"You'd better not," said Ginger, but William was already half-way up the cellar steps.

Ginger followed, his face tensed in anxiety.

In the hall William paused for a moment listening. The voices still continued outside the closed front door. Suddenly there was the sound of a key being turned in the lock.

"Quick!" gasped William.

He grabbed Ginger by the arm and drew him behind the oak chest.

The front door opened and two men entered. One was Police-Constable Higgs, an officer well known to William and Ginger, the other a young man whom William and Ginger had never seen before.

"What did you say you heard?" said the young man.

"Two revolver shots," said P.C. Higgs. "I was passing the gate and I heard them—plain as plain could

THE FRONT DOOR OPENED AND TWO MEN ENTERED. ONE WAS P.C. HIGGS, THE OTHER A YOUNG MAN WHOM WILLIAM AND GINGER HAD NEVER SEEN BEFORE.

be. Two revolver shots coming from this house. I knew it was supposed to be an empty house——"

"Of course it's an empty house," said the young man. He was fair and slight with an abrupt manner and a high-pitched voice. "It's my house. It belonged to my uncle and he left it to me when he died quite recently. There's a housekeeper but she's away at present."

"I know," said P.C. Higgs. "We've been told to keep an eye on it an' I was keepin' an eye on it when I heard those two revolver shots just now . . . Perhaps we should search the house, sir."

"We shall have to go very carefully," said the young man. "As a matter of fact I'm not at all surprised to hear of those revolver shots. There are plots and counter plots at work. I think I'd better tell you the whole story."

"Perhaps you had, sir," said P.C. Higgs, glancing nervously around.

P.C. Higgs was not a man to court danger, but he was a conscientious officer of the law and had accustomed himself to take what came to him with as little fuss as possible.

"Well," began the young man, "my uncle's most treasured possession was a few bars of a string quartet, written and signed by Haydn himself. He always said that he had left it to me in his will and meantime was keeping it in a safe hiding-place which he would reveal to me in due course. But the old chap popped off suddenly before he'd had time to do anything about it. I hadn't given much thought to the matter till I was approached by an American who'd heard about it and offered me two hundred pounds for the manuscript. And now I can't find the darn thing anywhere. I've searched the place through and can't find a trace. I've come along today just to have one more look. A sort of last hope."

"But—but the revolver shots, sir," said P.C. Higgs.

"Oh yes," said the young man, lowering his voice. "I've thought for some time that there was probably more than one collector after the thing. I was reading a book only last night with something of the same idea. Two men after the same bit of loot and they both went to the house where it was hidden and met unexpectedly and—well, there was a regular shooting match."

P.C. Higgs' usually ruddy countenance had paled. "Perhaps we ought to get help, sir," he said.

"We'd better await developments," said the young man. He entered the sitting-room, followed by the constable. "Yes, they've been at work here all right. Even searched the chimney for a hiding place. It's clear that we're up against professionals. Pity you haven't a revolver with you."

"Yes, sir," said P.C. Higgs. "Yes, indeed."

"We'll have a good look round," said the young man. He flung open the kitchen door. "Good Lord! This place has been simply *ransacked*. Just *look*! Groceries turned out of their containers and scattered broadcast. They weren't going to overlook any possible hiding place. I've heard of people hiding valuables in rice and sugar jars and so on. It's quite an old trick . . . Well, we'll try upstairs now shall we?"

"If—if you like, sir," said P.C. Higgs.

"You've heard no movement up there since we came in, have you?"

"No, sir."

"Just those two shots?"

"Yes, sir."

"Odd that we've heard no further sounds."

"Yes, sir."

"They may, of course, have hit each other in vital spots simultaneously . . . but I suppose that's hardly likely."

"No, sir."

"It may possibly have been a couple of back-fires from the road."

"Yes, sir," said the constable. He seemed to accept the explanation with relief.

"Well, let's make our way upstairs."

Their footsteps were heard ascending the staircase. Their voices came muted from the upper regions.

Slowly and painfully William and Ginger arose from their cramped positions behind the chest. They stared at each other dazedly.

"Let's get out quick," said William. "Look! The front door's open an' they're upstairs." He darted out of the house, ran a few yards down the drive then darted back again. "They're standin' at the upstairs window," he panted. "They can't help seein' us if we go down to the gate."

"Let's get behind the chest again," said Ginger.

"No," said William. "We've got to get out while the door's open. If they come down an' shut it an' go away we'll be locked in again. Come on. Let's get behind this bush, quick. They'll never see us there."

The two plunged behind a sturdy hydrangea that grew by the front door.

"It's a jolly good hiding-place," said William. "I vote we stay here till they've gone. It's a long way down to the gate an' they'll be sure to see us out of one of the windows if they're in the house an' then ole Higgs'll be on our track."

"All right," said Ginger resignedly.

William had raised his head from the bush and was gazing with interest at the car that stood at the door.

"It's got a funny sort of safety belt," he said. "I'm goin' to have a look at it."

"You *can't*, William," protested Ginger. "They'll *see* you."

"No, they won't," said William. "It's too close underneath them. They'd see us goin' down the drive, but they wouldn't see us right underneath the window, 'cept they've got eyes in their chins."

He approached the car, opened the door and inspected the belt.

"No, it's jus' an ordin'ry one," he said. "A bit posher than most of 'em, that's all"

But there had been a shopping basket full of parcels on the seat and the sweeping gestures with which William had carried out his examination of the safety belt had dislodged the basket and sent its contents—lettuce, loaf, packet of tea and bag of cherries—rolling over the drive.

"Gosh!" moaned Ginger helplessly.

"'S all right," said William. "I can pick 'em up." He put lettuce, loaf, tea and half-emptied bag of cherries back into the basket, replaced it on the seat and closed the door. "There's some cherries dropped out, but I bet he won't notice."

"But look at all those cherries on the ground," said Ginger. "They'll see 'em an' start gettin' suspicious ..."

"We'll pick 'em up an' put 'em in our pockets," said William. "They're too dirty to put back into the bag, anyway. It won't take a minute . . ."

Quickly they stuffed their pockets with the fallen cherries and returned to the shelter of the hydrangea bush.

"We might as well eat 'em," said William. "No good wastin' 'em."

"What is it they're lookin' for?" said Ginger, putting a cherry into his mouth. "I couldn't make it out, could you?"

"Bars of something," said William, wiping a dusty cherry on his pullover before eating it. "Sounded like string."

"Couldn't have been," said Ginger. "Not bars of string. It might've been balls of string or bars of choc'late. . . ."

"*Couldn't* have been," said William. "No one'd pay two hundred pounds for a ball of string *or* a bar of choc'late."

"It might be a code word," said Ginger.

"Yes, I bet that's it. Smugglers or international crooks," said William. "Bars of string might mean gold or diamonds or some sort of dangerous drugs."

"Funny we didn't find it, whatever it was," said Ginger. "We looked everywhere—tryin' to escape."

"I bet it was in that clergyman's secret room. I wish I'd gone through to it."

They ate cherries in silence for some time then turned their heads sharply towards the house, frozen to attention.

Through the open door they could hear footsteps descending the staircase . . . then voices in the hall.

"Oh, well," the young man was saying, "no corpses, no Haydn. A complete blank all round. Obviously someone's been searching the whole place—cupboards, drawers, everything. They've probably found it and are well away by now. Of course, there's always the possibility that the old chap sold it before he died or even invented the whole thing . . . Well, I think I'll take myself off now . . . Good Lord! That's queer."

"What's queer, sir,?" said P.C. Higgs.

"That hydrangea by the door. All the blooms are blue except one that seems to be a sort of orange. I'm a bit short-sighted, but—do you see what I mean? A kind of botanical freak, I suppose."

"More like a human boy, sir, from what I can see," said P.C. Higgs.

He plunged a hand into the bush, caught hold of a tuft of Ginger's hair and drew him up to the surface. William followed more slowly.

The young man turned on them in fury.

"What do you mean, trespassing on my property?" he shouted.

William assumed the imbecile expression that he used to denote innocence.

"We were jus' doin' a bit of nature study," he said blandly. "We didn't think we were doin' any harm, jus' doin' a bit of nature study."

"Jus' a bit of birds-nestin'," said Ginger in further explanation.

"Shut up, you clot!" said William.

"Birds-*nesting*!" almost screamed the young man. He was feeling disappointed and irritated by his failure to find the missing legacy and was glad of a legitimate outlet for his anger. "Birds-nesting in a hydrangea bush! I never heard such nonsense! What sort of birds, do you think, nest in hydrangea bushes?"

"That's what we were trying to find out," said William, fixing him with a blank unwinking stare. "That's what we were nature-studyin' about. We were tryin' to find what sort of birds nested in hydrangea bushes. We——"

"Be *quiet,*" roared the young man. "How *dare* you come here making hay of a valuable shrub like this!" His eyes lighted suddenly on the front door steps. William and Ginger had flipped their cherry stones carelessly about them and the doorsteps were freely bespattered with them. "How *dare* you leave your filthy litter all over my grounds! I might have slipped over them. I might have broken my neck."

"But you haven't," William pointed out reassuringly.

"The disgusting sight of those beastly cherry stones and mangled cherries——"

"Some of 'em were a bit bad so's we could only eat bits of 'em," explained William."

"—make me *sick,*" continued the young man.

"Well, look," said William pacifically. "I'm sorry we put 'em there, but I'll clear 'em all away so they'll stop makin' you sick. I've got a bit of paper in my pocket an' I'll pick 'em all up an' wrap them in this bit of paper an' take 'em right away an' bury 'em somewhere."

He took the piece of paper from his pocket, laid it on the doorstep, and began to collect the cherry stones.

The young man's face turned from purple to green. His mouth dropped open. His eyes bulged.

"S-s-s-stop!" he said. "Where did you find that paper?"

"Diggin' a tunnel in the cellar," said William.

"'Stead of a wooden horse," added Ginger in further explanation.

The young man had swooped down and seized the paper, sending cherry stones flying in all directions.

William felt that the moment had come to make good his escape.

"Come on!" he said to Ginger and they started at a run down the drive.

"Come back!" shouted the young man. "Come *back*, I tell you! Catch them, Officer! *Catch* them!"

The young man and P.C. Higgs set off in pursuit, each making for a different gate. William, finding his way barred by the constable, dodged round him, tripped him up and ran down the road, closely followed by Ginger. Rounding a bend that hid them from their pursuers, they plunged into the ditch that bordered the roadside and crouched there motionless. The young man and P.C. Higgs stood for a few moments at the bend of the road, nonplussed.

"Where are they?" said the young man.

P.C. Higgs shook his head sadly.

"One never knows with them young limbs," he said.

"Why? Do you know them?"

"'Oo doesn't?" asked P.C. Higgs bitterly.

"Oh, well, I can go and see their fathers later and get the thing sorted out. At present it's completely wrapped in mystery, but I must put this paper into the hands of my lawyer at once before any further mishap occurs."

"Then you won't need me any more, sir?" said P.C. Higgs, brightening.

"I don't think so. Those shots you heard must have been back-fires or any normal country sound—cocks or owls or something."

"Yes, sir," said P.C. Higgs.

Henry and Douglas were walking slowly down the road towards Meadowview. At the bend of the road they stopped and looked at the house that showed through a gap in the trees.

"I can't see either of them, can you?" said Henry.

"No," said Douglas.

Then a movement behind them startled them and they turned to see two bedraggled figures crawling out of the ditch.

"William!" said Henry.

"Ginger!" said Douglas.

"Have they gone?" said William, looking cautiously around.

"They seem to've done," said Ginger.

Henry and Douglas were still gazing in fascinated horror at William. William was the more bedraggled of the two. The day's activities had all left their marks on his person, and his sojourn in the ditch had added a few finishing touches. His hair stood up in stiff spikes, his jacket was torn, his tie adrift, his face and legs coated in soot and mud.

"Gosh!" said Henry." Whatever's happened?"

William's mind went back over the scenes of his morning's escapade . . . the assault on the chimney, the chaos of the kitchen, the flooding of the bathroom; the cellar, the tunnel, the ginger beer, the hydrangea bush.

But they all paled into insignificance beside the one outstanding fact.

"What's happened?" he repeated. "Can't you *see* what's happened?" A triumphant grin irradiated his grubby features.

"We've GOT OUT!"

IV

WILLIAM AND THE HOLIDAY TASK

WILLIAM had paid little attention to the holiday task till a week before term began.

It was the first time the form had been given a holiday task. Mr. French, their form master, did not approve of holiday tasks; he considered that they imposed an undue strain on both master and pupil at a time—the beginning of term—when they were least able to bear it. He had occasionally been tempted to set his pupils the task of committing to memory *The Ancient Mariner* or *John Gilpin*—poems that, he considered, every educated person should know by heart—but had always been restrained by the sobering thought that he would have to hear them say it. But last term Mr. French had had to retire from public life in order to undergo an operation and his place had been taken by Mr. Mostyn, a flamboyant youth with a startling taste in socks and ties, whose "modern" methods of teaching left the minds of his pupils completely but not unpleasantly befogged.

In point of fact, Mr. Mostyn made few demands on his pupils. He was so deeply engrossed in acting the part of unconventional schoolmaster to his own satisfaction that he required little or no support from the rest of the cast. When, on the last day of term, he announced a holiday task the Outlaws, seated together in the back row and engaged in trying to teach Henry's tortoise to stand on its hind legs, did not even realise that a holiday task was being set.

As the holidays progressed, however, details of the task reached them. They were told that the pupils were expected to find objects of local interest, archaeological or historical, with a view to forming a "museum," but, occupied in their own concerns (which included fixing up a secret radio in the old quarry to catch smugglers and constructing a submarine to navigate the village pond), they received the information with indifference. Details of the various "finds", too, filtered through to them. These consisted chiefly of flints, old coins, old prints and old photographs. Many of the "flints" bore a striking likeness to ordinary pebbles, and many of the old photographs were of comparative recent date, showing, for example, Ella Poppleham winning the sack race at the Liberal Association Summer Fête and the Over Sixty Club setting out for a jaunt to Coventry Cathedral, complete with cameras, Thermos flasks, knitting, transistors and guide-books.

Some, however, were definitely worthy of respect. Victor Jameson's flint had been pronounced authentic by a cousin who had once been on a "dig", Peter Clayton's coin (salvaged from the Roman Villa at Mellings) bore the word ROMA plainly incised and Hubert Lane's map had mail coach roads marked instead of railways.

It was not till their usual occupations began to pall that the Outlaws turned their attention to the holiday task.

"They've got a lot of rubbish for it," said William as the four wandered somewhat aimlessly over the fields. "Bits of stone an' ole pennies an' photographs of people no one wants to see photographs of. Gosh! I bet we could have found somethin' better than those ole things if we'd tried."

"Well, why didn't we?" said Ginger.

"'Cause we'd got other things to do," said William.

"Well, we've done them," said Douglas. "We couldn't find any smugglers and the submarine wouldn't surface."

"It's too late to do that ole holiday thing now, anyway," said William.

"No, it isn't," said Henry. "Term doesn't start till next Thursday. That gives us a whole week."

"An' I bet we can find somethin' a jolly sight more interestin' than stones an' pennies an' snapshots an' that ole map of Hubert's in a whole week," said William.

Suddenly and rather to their surprise, they found themselves committed to the holiday task. Their spirits rose and the shadow of boredom that had begun to hang over them vanished.

"We'll have to work jolly hard an' jolly fast," said Henry.

"Huh! We can do that all right," said William.

"Yes, there's four of us," said Ginger, "an' he said we could do it in groups."

They had reached the old barn and, sitting down on the ground in the doorway in a patch of sunlight, they stared thoughtfully in front of them.

"We'll have somethin' diff'rent from any of their things," said William, "*an'* a jolly sight more int'restin'."

"Yes, but what?"

"We ought to have somethin'—archaeological," said Henry, bringing the word out with a modest air of knowledge. "Somethin' dug up out of the past that's been in the earth for hundreds of years."

"Yes, but *what?*"

"There was somethin' in the newspaper once," said Henry thoughtfully. "It was dug up in London. It was a head."

"What sort of a head?" said Ginger.

"It was a head called ——" Henry pondered for a moment or two, then continued: "Yes, I remember now. It was called Mithras."

"Never heard of him," said William. "He couldn't have been anyone much."

"It was a heathen god that people used to worship," said Henry, "an' it was jolly important. There were pictures of it in the newspapers. It was hundreds of years old."

William's interest was quickening.

"Where did they find it?" he said.

"They found it when they were diggin' a hole in the road in London near the Post Office. There was a picture of that, too."

"But—gosh!" said William excitedly. "They're diggin' a hole in the road near the Post Office here. Come on! Let's go an' have a look."

"They'll have stopped diggin' now," said Douglas. "It's after five an' they stop at five."

"Well, we can go an' have a look," said William.

They crossed the field and walked down the road to the Post Office. The road outside was "up", and the workmen had gone. The hole was enclosed by a circle of posts joined by rope, with lanterns set at intervals. They stood looking down into the hole.

"I don't see anythin' there," said Douglas.

"I 'spect they had to dig down a bit to get at that head in London," said Henry.

"Well, I'll have a bash at it," said William. He looked up and down the road. "No one's comin'." He ducked under the rope and disappeared into the hole. "No, there's nothin' here but I'll jus' dig about a bit." After a few moments his voice came again, upraised excitedly. "Yes, there is somethin' an'—gosh! It's a *head*! . . . I'm goin' to throw it up to you. Get hold of it quick!"

A rounded object was hurled out of the hole. Henry seized it and took it to the side of the road. They stood around examining it. Though discoloured by clay, it was certainly a head. The hair was set in curls, the lips into a half-smile.

"Yes, it's the head of an ancient statue of a heathen god all right," said Henry with the air of an expert. "I hope it's not the sort that brings a curse."

"A what?" said William, emerging from his hole to join them.

"A curse," said Henry. "Same as mummies. I read about a mummy once that someone dug up an' ghastly trag'dies kept happenin' to everyone who'd had anythin' to do with diggin' it up. An' they went on happenin' till they put it back where they found it."

"Gosh!" said William, startled by this idea.

"Yes, an' I once saw a picture about someone who took a jewel out of a heathen grave an' awful things kept happenin' to him till he put it back."

"Well, it's not a mummy or a jewel," said William, "so we needn't worry."

"An' it looks kind," said Douglas, examining the face that smirked up at them through its coating of clay.

"YES, IT'S THE HEAD OF AN ANCIENT STATUE OF A HEATHEN GOD ALL RIGHT," SAID HENRY.

"It hasn't any eyes," said Ginger.

"Statues don't have," said Henry.

Douglas glanced nervously up and down the road.

"Let's take it away quick," he said. "We don't want anyone to catch us with it."

"All right. Let's go back to the old barn," said William.

In the old barn they set their 'find' on the ground and inspected it closely.

"It's the best I've ever seen," said William. "I 'spect they'll want it for the British Museum."

"We won't let them have it yet," said Henry.

"No," agreed William. "We don't want anyone to see it till we take it to school nex' Thursday. Gosh! Think of Hubert's face when he sees it. It'll make his ole map look pretty silly."

"Yes, but what are we goin' to do with it till Thursday?" said Ginger. "We've got to keep it hidden somewhere where no one'll see it."

"I'll take it home with me," said William. "I know some good hiding-places."

"But how are you goin' to *get* it there?" said Ginger. "You can't walk through the village carryin' a heathen god's statue's head. Everyone'd see it an' start gettin' nosey."

William considered.

"Tell you what!" he said. "I'll go home an' fetch a a bag to put it in. There's a lot of old sacks in the tool-shed that my father's had garden stuff in. I'll bring one of those."

"All right," said Henry. "We'll stay here an' guard it."

William set off briskly down the road. There was a

faraway look in his eyes, a jaunty swagger in his walk. He was being fêted and acclaimed as the discoverer of the most sensational archaeological find of the century. Scholars and professors of the highest standing showered congratulations on him. Fantastic offers flowed in to him from America, but he refused them and presented the head to the British Museum. The British Museum was ecstatically grateful and held a banquet in his honour, giving three cheers for him at the end. He was knighted and his photograph—Sir William Brown—appeared in all the papers. Reporters flocked to interview him. A modest smile curved his lips as he kicked a stone across the road. "Well, it was sort of luck in a way," he was saying. "I mean, I've got a sort of *instinct*. I jus' looked at that hole an' I *knew* it had got a heathen god's statue's head in it. I——"

Absorbed in his dreams, he collided with Archie Mannister coming from the opposite direction. Archie Mannister was a local artist whose fame was limited to his immediate circle and who cherished a burning—and so far unrequited—passion for William's sister, Ethel. Though Archie lacked William's force of character and, in any case, belonged to the adult world, the two had a certain amount in common. Both were driven by vaulting ambitions that life had as yet failed to satisfy, and fate had a way of landing both of them in strange and unexpected situations.

"Hello, Archie," said William.

Archie hurried on without looking at him or speaking. His eyes were glassy, his brow furrowed. Even his short red beard seemed to be quivering with some uncontrollable emotion.

William stood in the road gazing after him.

"Oh, all right," he muttered aggrievedly. "I was goin' to tell him about that head but I won't now."

He found a suitably sized bag of green sacking in a corner of the tool-shed. It had contained garden peat and was only a little larger than the head. He carried it back to the old barn and placed the head in it. The four set off for William's house. An air of solemnity hung over them.

"You'll have to—watch out a bit, you know," said Henry. "It might turn nasty like that mummy I read about. It doesn't *look* the sort that would set curses on you, but that mummy in the picture had a sort of smile on its face, too."

William slowed his pace.

"Isn't there any way of stopping them?" he said. "Curses, I mean."

"I dunno," said Henry vaguely. "They used to put food in mummies' graves in ancient times to keep 'em happy, an' they used to offer sacrifices to heathen gods . . . But I 'spect it'll be all right."

"Anyway, it's goin' to make us famous," said William. "We won't let anyone see it till after Thursday an' after that we'll let the British Museum come an' have a look at it."

They were passing Archie's cottage. Douglas stopped.

"Let's go 'n' see if Archie's got any sweets," he said.

Archie had a way of buying packets of boiled sweets and then losing interest in them. He was generally glad to hand over a few sodden little packets of melting sugar to the Outlaws.

"He's not there," said William. "I met him goin' along the road to Hadley. He was jus' glarin' in front of him an' he didn't seem to see me at all."

"He was prob'ly gettin' an idea for a picture," said Henry. "That's the way they get ideas, artists. He's probably sittin' in a wood now, paintin' like mad."

But Archie was not sitting in a wood painting like mad. He was standing in the studio of Hadley Art School talking to Miss Stanton, a member of the staff, whose modelling classes he had been attending for the past few weeks. His face was drawn with anguish and he accompanied his words with sweeping gestures that seemed to agitate his whole body.

"It's the best thing I've ever done," he was saying, "and—and—well, I just can't understand it."

"What exactly has happened, Mr. Mannister?" said Miss Stanton patiently.

"I'm trying to tell you," said Archie. "You see, I did this head of Ethel——"

"Your girl friend?"

"Y-yes . . . I mean, she's more my girl friend than I'm her boy friend, if you know what I mean. I mean, she's never taken me seriously, but I hoped this head I did of her would show her something of what I felt for her and—and show her something of my artistic ability. It was the best thing I've ever done. I put my new signature on it, too."

"Your——?"

"My new signature. Like Whistler's butterfly. Didn't I tell you? I've decided in future to stamp all my work with an acorn. It's a symbol of artistic growth." He stopped and looked at her helplessly. "Or isn't it?"

Miss Stanton sighed.

"Mr. Mannister, I'm rather busy today. Perhaps you could get to the point."

MISS STANTON SIGHED. "MR MANNISTER, I'M RATHER BUSY TODAY. PERHAPS YOU COULD GET TO THE POINT."

"I'm trying to," said Archie. "Honestly I am. You see, I'd finished this head. Quite the best thing I've ever done. And I was bringing it to you so that you might perhaps suggest some further touches to make it more perfect. A spot of colour perhaps. Like the old masters. Della Robbia, for instance . . ."

"*Please,* Mr. Mannister!"

"I'm telling you as quickly as I can," said Archie in dignified reproach. "Well, I was carrying it along the road when suddenly I saw Ethel coming from the opposite direction. I didn't want her to see the head just then. I could hardly present it to her in the middle of the village street, and I couldn't hide it because the piece of paper I'd put round it was very inadequate so——"

"Yes?" said Miss Stanton.

"Well, I was passing an excavation in the road and on a sudden impulse I slipped the head into it and pushed the soil down over it with my foot. I meant to get it out as soon as she'd passed, but it turned out that she was taking some things in a suitcase for her mother to the Village Hall for a jumble sale, so of course I had to carry it for her—I mean, I considered it a *privilege* to carry it for her—and when I got back to the hole—well, you simply won't believe this——"

"The head had gone," said Miss Stanton.

Archie gaped at her.

"How did you know?" he said.

"It seemed to be the inevitable *dénouement*," said Miss Stanton wearily. "The whole story seemed to be leading up to it. How do you account for the loss?"

"I can't," said Archie. "I've been thinking and thinking about it ever since it happened. I—I wondered . . ."

"Yes, Mr. Mannister?"

The tension of Archie's features had relaxed into an expression that was almost sheepish.

"It's honestly the best thing I've ever done . . . I just wondered . . . I mean, it occurred to me that—well, it really *is* the best thing I've ever done and I thought—I mean, the idea came into my mind that perhaps some—some unprincipled art collector might have seen it (you can see right into the studio of my cottage from the road, you know) and followed me and

—well, you do hear of such things, you know. I suppose —I suppose it's possible."

"I hardly think so, Mr. Mannister," said Miss Stanton.

"Oh . . ." said Archie.

It didn't take much to deflate Archie. He collapsed like a pricked balloon.

Miss Stanton looked at him. She was tired of Archie. She was tired of teaching him modelling. She was tired of his earnestness, his futility, his pathos. An idea occurred to her.

"Do you know, Mr. Mannister," she said, "I think that Neo-primitive art is really more in your line."

"What's that?" said Archie.

"It's a form of art that breaks away from tradition altogether," she said. "You just draw as a child or a savage might draw. From the subconscious, as it were. It's very popular just now."

"Oh . . ." said Archie again.

"I think it's just down your street, Mr. Mannister. I think you'd find that you had a real gift for it."

Archie brightened.

"Do you really?" he said.

"I do indeed," said Miss Stanton. She too had brightened. "Mr. Jenkins holds a class on Neo-primitive art every Wednesday evening."

Archie's face clouded over again. On Wednesday evenings Ethel went to the Country Dancing class and he always accompanied her, to carry the bag containing her country dancing outfit to and from the Village Hall.

"On Wednesdays . . ." he said. "I'm not sure about Wednesdays."

"Well, think about it," said Miss Stanton.

"Yes, I'll think about it."

"And don't worry about the head."

"I'll try not to," said Archie.

Henry, Ginger and Douglas were looking anxiously from the doorway of the old barn the next morning when William approached it. His face was set and stern. He carried the small green sack.

"What have you brought it back for?" said Henry. "I thought you were goin' to keep it till Thursday."

"It's the curse," said William.

"The curse?"

"Yes. It's started workin' already. We've had an awful time with it."

"How?"

William set the sack down on the ground.

"It started last night. Gosh! You never saw anythin' like it. It was a ghastly trag'dy, all right."

"Well, what *was* it?"

"I'm tryin' to tell you if you wouldn't keep int'ruptin'. The shelf fell down."

"What shelf?"

"The shelf in the wardrobe of the spare room."

"Well, there's not much of a curse in that."

"Isn't there!" said William with a harsh laugh. "There was broken glass an' jam an' marmalade an' plums an' gooseberries all over the place. *With* all their juice!"

"Where did it all come from?" said Douglas.

"I keep *tellin'* you," said William impatiently. "From the shelf at the top of the wardrobe in the spare room. My mother had been keepin' all her jam an' bottled fruit there an' she'd put the chutney she'd made yesterday on it an' the whole thing fell down in the night. You never saw such a mess. She was in an awful state. She nearly cried. An' it was all my fault, hidin' that ole head under the spare room bed. It started its curse right away. Didn't even wait till the morning."

"It might have happened any other time," said Henry. "It needn't have been the curse."

"Well, it didn't happen any other time." said William. "Use a bit of sense. An' it couldn't have been anythin' *but* the curse. What else could it have been?"

"Gravity," suggested Henry tentatively after a moment's thought.

"Well, it wasn't gravity," said William. "It was the curse. I was there an' I ought to know. An' I can't have it in our house any longer. She said it'd only take one more thing like that to send her into a mental home."

"I think we'd better give up this head business altogether," said Douglas. "It's gettin' a bit dangerous."

"No, I don't want to give it up," said William. "I took a lot of trouble gettin' that head an' it's the best bit of local antiquity anyone's ever found round here. It's only the curse . . ."

"But what can you do about a curse?" said Douglas.

"Well, I'm the one that took it out of its hole," said William, "so I bet I'm the one it's after. I think it'd be all right if one of you took it."

"Let's have another look at it," said Ginger.

William's father had evidently failed to use the entire contents of the bag and through a covering of garden peat the empty eyes seemed to glare at them balefully. The faint smile had lost the suggestion of inane good nature that it had held the day before. It was mocking . . . evil . . . malicious.

"Doesn't look as nice as it did yesterday," said Douglas.

"It's only that stuff it's got on its face," said William. "It'll look better when we've washed it. Well, I can't take it back with me, so one of the rest of you'll have to take it."

"I will," said Henry. "I'll put it somewhere where it can't do any damage."

"All right," said William. "Find a good place for it an' it can stay there till Thursday."

But the next morning when they went to Henry's house he emerged from it furtively, carrying the small green sack.

"What have you brought it out for?" said William. "You were goin' to keep it till Thursday."

"Come to the old barn an' I'll tell you," said Henry, throwing a nervous glance behind him.

They hurried across the field to the old barn.

"Did your mother's jam fall down, too?" said William.

"No," said Henry. "It was worse. I hid it in the cupboard in the bathroom where the tank is. That's next to the nursery, you know, where our baby is, an' jus' a few minutes after I'd hid in there, it put the tail of its toy monkey into its mouth an' it stuck in its throat an' nearly choked it to death."

"What? The head?"

"No, you clot! The baby."

"Well, it didn't axshully choke it to death, did it?"

"No, 'cause my mother took it out, but it might have done if she'd not been there."

"It's always chokin' over things," said William. "It doesn't seem to have much sense."

"It's got a jolly sight more sense than most babies," said Henry with spirit. "It's on page seven of Mother's baby book an' for its age it ought to be only on page five."

Henry professed a scornful indifference to his baby sister but was apt to rise hotly to her defence when criticism was levelled at her by others.

"Anyway, it never axshully choked," said William, "an' I bet it'd have put that monkey's tail in its mouth anyway, even if the head hadn't been in the nex' room."

"Well, I'm not goin' to risk it," said Henry. "My mother thinks a lot of it. She'd be mad if anythin' happened to it."

"I think that baby of yours is jolly selfish," said Ginger. "Messin' everything up!"

"P'raps *you'd* like to keep that ole head for a bit, then?" said Henry aggressively.

"Yes, I wouldn't mind," said Ginger. "I'm not scared. Let's have a look at it."

"I washed it . . ." said Henry.

He drew the head from the bag. Though it had collected a fresh coating of garden peat from its sojourn in the bag, the face gleamed through it with a bone-like pallor.

"What's happened to its nose?" said William.

"I gave it a good scrub and a few bits of its nose came off," said Henry. "A few bits of its hair came off too."

"It's gettin' a nasty sort of look," said Ginger judicially.

"Yes, it is, rather," admitted William, "but p'raps it's used up its curse now. Or p'raps it doesn't like bein' indoors. Try keepin' it somewhere out of doors. I bet it won't do any harm out of doors. Anyway, you've not got a baby or jam on your wardrobe shelf, so you ought to be all right."

"Oh, I'm not scared of it," said Ginger again with a careless laugh.

But somehow they were not surprised to see him approaching the old barn the next morning with the familiar green sack in his hand.

"Gosh! What's it done now?" said William irritably.

"Well, I did what you said," said Ginger. "I put it out of doors. I put it in the frame in the garden right in the corner, 'cause I wanted it to keep dry 'case it rained. Anyway——"

"Yes? What happened?"

"Well, when we got up this mornin' a rabbit had got into the garden an' eaten all my father's lettuces. Every single one of them. Gosh! He was mad. It was a ghastly trag'dy same as yours. He'd raised them from seed an' planted them out an' watered them an' then it comes along an' eats every single one of them up."

"Well, the head hadn't eaten them," said William. "You talk as if the head had eaten them. You can't blame the *head*."

"Oh, can't I!" said Ginger. "I bet that rabbit wouldn't have come if that head hadn't been there."

"You've had rabbits in your garden before," said William. "You're bound to with the wood at the bottom of your garden."

"We've not had one for months an' *months*," said Ginger. "It was jolly funny it came jus' that day I'd got the head."

"Well, jus' try it another night," said William.

"No, I'm not goin' to," said Ginger. "I'm not goin' to have it eatin' any more stuff an' puttin' him in a worse temper than he is already. If it starts on his outdoor tomatoes he'll jus' go bonkers. He shot at it but he didn't hit it. He only scared it an' it ran off, but I bet if I took that head home again, it'd come back an' finish off the whole lot."

"Perhaps you didn't treat it right," said Douglas.

"I did everythin' I could think of," said Ginger. "I gave it some food same as Henry said they did to mummies to keep 'em happy. I gave it some tinned strawberries an' I broke a bit off its mouth tryin' to get some carrot into it."

He drew the head out of the sack. Its appearance had certainly changed for the worse. A bright red stain adorned its chin, and the broken mouth had lost all traces of its smile, showing a twisted malevolent snarl.

"You've made a mess of it all right," said William.

"Well, I'm not havin' it any more," said Ginger. "I'm not goin' to risk it. Eatin' every single one of his lettuces! We're not goin' to hear the last of it for years."

"You keep talkin' as if the *head* had eaten them," said William.

Ginger threw a glance at the disfigured object.

"I'm not sure it didn't," he said darkly.

William turned to Douglas.

"You'll have to take it, Douglas. It's your turn."

Douglas had been facing this moment ever since he saw Ginger returning with the bag. He had thought out various excuses and discarded them all as useless. He knew that he would have to accept the inevitable.

"All right," he said gloomily, "but if the worst comes

to the worst, I hope you'll always remember that you *made* me do it."

"Yes, we will," promised William, "but p'raps it'll have got used to goin' about with us by now. I 'spect it was jus' that it was a bit homesick at first."

"Funny sort of homesick!" said Douglas with a bitter laugh. "I was homesick when I stayed with my aunt, but I didn't go about smashin' people's jam jars an' chokin' their babies an' eatin' up their lettuces . . ."

"Never mind," said William. "It's only for a few days. It can't do much damage in a few days."

"Can't it!" said Douglas with another bitter laugh.

"Anyway, we've jus' *got* to have it for this holiday task, now we've taken all this trouble," said William.

"Frankie Dakers has got an ancient oyster shell from the rubbish heap of that Roman villa," said Henry.

"An' Jimmy Barlow's got a photograph of the church before they put in the War Memorial window," said Ginger.

"Well, that's *nothin'* compared with a real heathen god's statue's head," said William. "It'll be the best of the whole lot."

"What's left of it," said Douglas.

"Well—gosh, ancient things have got to be a bit knocked about. They wouldn't be ancient if they weren't. I bet the British Museum wouldn't even *look* at anythin' that wasn't knocked about . . . Go on, Douglas. I bet it'll settle down quietly at your house."

"All right," said Douglas gloomily. He threw a glance of disfavour at his charge. "I suppose I might try offerin' it a sacrifice . . ."

They watched him as he went across the field, holding the bag as far as possible away from his person.

"I bet it'll be all right now," said William with never-failing optimism.

The next morning they stood at the doorway of the old barn waiting for him in anxious silence. At last his figure was seen in the distance.

"He's not got it," cried William triumphantly.

But, as Douglas drew nearer, the swelling beneath his coat showed that he was carrying it carefully concealed.

"Well, you've not kept it long," said William as he reached them. There was a note of cold condemnation in his voice.

"I've kept it as long as the rest of you did," said Douglas, drawing the green sack from his coat and placing it on the ground. "I kept it as long as I poss'bly could. I only jus' escaped with my life. I bet my trag'dy's the ghastliest of the whole lot."

"Why? What did it do to *you*?"

"Pushed me off the roof."

"Pushed you——?"

"Pushed me off the roof. I wanted to get up to my bedroom without anyone seein' the head, an' my mother was in the sittin'-room where she'd have seen me comin' in with it at the gate, so I went round to the back gate an' round to the back garden an' I stuck the head up under my pullover an' got on the fence to climb up the kitchen roof into my bedroom window an' I'd hardly got on to the roof when I fell right down."

"You've often fallen off that roof before."

"Yes, but not as badly as this time. I've still got the bruises. It was the curse, all right."

"Well, it wasn't as bad as breakin' jam jars an' chokin' babies an' turnin' rabbits loose in people's gardens. Where did you put it in the end?"

"In the garage behind the oil drum an' I shouldn't be surprised if there's somethin' wrong with the car the next time my father wants to take it out."

"Did you try offerin' it a sacrifice?"

"Yes, I did. There was a fire at the bottom of the garden that the gard'ner had started an' it was still burnin' an' I put the head at the side of it an' I burnt my last year's pocket diary for a sacrifice."

"I don't call that a sacrifice," said Henry.

"It was near enough," said Douglas. "It wouldn't know it was last year's."

"I bet it did," said Ginger. "It knows everything."

"Anyway, I'm sorry I burnt it now. I'd kept it 'cause it told you how gliders were made an' I thought it might come in useful. An' all that head did back was to push me off the roof."

"Well, I think you might have kept it a bit longer," said William.

"I couldn't now, anyway," said Douglas, "'cause my mother's gettin' suspicious. She saw me takin' it out this mornin' an' she said, 'What have you got in that bag?' an' when I said 'Nothin',' she said it was a funny shape for nothin', an' I bet if I take it back she'll be on to it . . . I like her," he added as an afterthought, "but she's a bit nosey."

"Well," said William in a tone of finality, "we'll jus' have to find somewhere else to keep it. It's no use havin' it in any of our houses 'cause we've tried."

"What about the ditch?" said Henry. "It couldn't do any harm in a ditch."

They turned to look at the ditch that ran between the field and the hedge.

"Yes, that's a good idea," said William. "It's a sort of hole, too. It might feel more at home there."

"Let's take it out of the bag," said Ginger. "P'raps it doesn't like bein' in a bag."

Douglas drew the head from its bag and set it on the ground.

"Gosh!" said William. "Whatever have you done to it this time? It gets worse every time it comes out."

"It's only the smoke from the sacrifice," explained Douglas. "The wind was blowin' in its direction. I 'spect it'll wash off."

"We'll jus' stick it in the ditch, then," said William. "We can wash it afterwards. We won't put it back in its bag. P'raps it doesn't like bein' in a bag. It wasn't in a bag in its hole . . . Come on."

It was a dry ditch, overgrown with weeds and grass. William placed the head at the bottom, carefully covering it with long grass.

Old Amos Faversham, one of Farmer Jenks's labourers, was cutting the hedge by the gate when they reached it. He gave them a cheery wave of his bagging hook and a "Hello, young 'uns" as they passed. They walked slowly down the road.

"If it's all right tomorrow," said William, "we can leave it there till Thursday. Call for me first thing tomorrow mornin' an' we'll go an' have a look at it."

Next morning their families were mildly surprised by the alacrity with which they rose and the scanty appetites they showed for breakfast.

"I'm jus' not hungry," said William impatiently, as he hastily swallowed a few spoonfuls of cereal and made for the door. "There isn't any *law* about bein' hungry, is there?"

He hurried out of the house and down to the gate, where Ginger, Henry and Douglas awaited him.

"It's sure to be all right," he said, as they made their way down the road. "It can't have done more than kill a few nettles, anyway."

Amos was already at work on the hedge when they reached the field. He looked less cheerful than he had looked the day before.

"Well, young 'uns," he said, "an' how do you find yourselves this mornin'?"

"Very well, thank you, Mr. Faversham," said Henry. "How do you find yourself?"

Henry was a stickler for etiquette, a sayer of "How d'you do," an inquirer after people's health. He steered his way with easy skill through the complexities of social usage.

"All right, thankee, except for me rheumatics," said Amos. "They've come on somethin' cru'l this mornin'. Sign of rain, I suppose."

They stared at him in silent dismay.

"I'm so sorry, Mr. Faversham," said Henry, recovering himself with an effort.

They began to make their way across the field, their faces set and anxious.

"'Course it's not a sign of rain," said Ginger.

"No, it's the curse all right," said William. "He's been doin' that bit jus' near where the head is."

"If he dies of rheumatics," said Henry, "we'll have his death on our hands."

"An' he's got a wife an' fam'ly," said Douglas. "They'll miss him."

They peered down half fearfully into the ditch at the

spot where they had left the head. It leered up at them through the tangled grass.

"Well, what are we goin' to do with it *now*?" said Ginger.

"Let's chuck it in the dustbin," said Douglas.

"An' what about the poor ole dustman an' *his* wife an' family?" said William indignantly. "He's a jolly nice man, too. He was in the Navy in the war an' he's got a jellyfish tattoed on his chest."

"Well, what *are* we goin' to do, then?" said Henry.

"There's only one thing to do," said William. "You said those things carried on with their curses till they were put back in the places they'd been taken from, so we'll jus' have to put this head back in its hole."

"But what about the holiday task?" said Henry.

"We can't help that," said William. "We can't go on startin' ghastly trag'dies all over the place like this."

"It's a miracle I'm not dead," said Douglas gloomily. "You should see the colour of my bruise this mornin'."

"Oh, shut up about your bruise," said William. "We're not interested in your bruise. Where's the bag?"

Douglas drew the bag from his pocket. Carefully they replaced the head.

"It seemed to grin at me," said Ginger.

"I thought it winked," said Henry.

"Oh, come on!" said William.

They made their way to the Post Office. The stretch of road outside was smooth and unbroken. Workmen were packing equipment into a lorry.

"Gosh! Have you filled it in?" said William.

"Yes . . . Job finished," said one of the men.

"You couldn't—you couldn't jus' open it up again

jus' for a minute or two, could you?" said William, an unusual note of diffidence in his voice.

"I could *not*," said the man. "Why?"

"Oh nothin'," said William despondently.

The four turned and trailed off down the road. Suddenly William stopped.

"I've got an idea," he said.

They looked at him with dawning hope.

"What is it?"

"Well, Colonel Masters is havin' an exhibition of his brother's African curios this afternoon. His brother's come home from Africa an' brought a lot of curios with him an' he's stayin' with Colonel Masters till he gets a house an' Colonel Masters is havin' an exhibition of his things this afternoon an' he's asked everyone to go to it."

"Yes, I know," said Henry. "He's asked my family."

"An' mine," said Ginger.

"An' mine," said Douglas.

"Well, I heard someone talkin' about it an' he's got a lot of witch doctors' masks," said William, "an' witch doctors have the strongest magic in the world. I bet a heathen god's head's magic's *nothin'* to a witch doctor's magic. . . . Well, listen. We'll go to this exhibition with our families, an' we'll slip this head in with the witch doctors' masks an' I bet their magic'll kill this ole head's magic right off. I bet there won't be any of it left."

They considered the suggestion doubtfully.

"It might work," said Henry, "an' it might not."

"All right. You think of somethin' better," challenged William. "You think of somethin' that won't go breakin' jam jars an' chokin' babies an' pushin' people off roofs an' eatin' lettuces. Go on. Think of it." Henry frowned thoughtfully and remained silent. "All right, then, that's what we'll do. We'll get that ditch stuff an' sacrifice stuff off its face an' slip it in with the witch doctors' masks till its magic's gone, then we'll fetch it away an' it'll make a jolly good holiday task."

As usual they found themselves infected by William's optimism.

"It's worth tryin'," said Henry.

"'Course it is," said William.

Colonel Masters' library was crowded with the guests who had come to see his brother's collection of African curios. Most of the guests had assembled at one end of the room where Colonel Masters was explaining that his brother had been called away on business, but had arranged the collection before his departure. He then proceeded to give a short account of his brother's journeys and adventures in South Africa.

The Outlaws had sloped into the room, each behind his own family, and had then furtively gathered together round a table in a small recess on which the witch doctors' masks were displayed. William's eyes rested on them in silent satisfaction. They were towering and terrifying, with monstrous painted features and expressions of hideous ferocity. There would be little left of the head's magic, he thought, after a sojourn in their company.

Henry carried the head in his school satchel (Henry's parents were notoriously vague and had accepted his explanation that he was "takin' somethin' somewhere" without question) and the other three closed round him to shield him from view as he drew out the head and placed it among the masks. They then wandered over to the opposite side of the room to gaze with eager—and slightly over-acted—interest at the photograph of an elephant shot by Colonel Masters' brother in 1910.

Colonel Masters had finished his little lecture and the guests spread out over the room. The largest group gathered round the table that held the witch doctors' masks.

William turned to watch the scene. Yes, already the head seemed to have shrunk. Its barely discernible features had lost their expression of malicious triumph. The faint twisted smile was apologetic, almost cringing. The thing wore a beaten, defeated air.

"It looks scared," he whispered to Ginger.

"Serve it right!" said Ginger.

General Moult was peering with dim, short-sighted eyes at the masks.

"What's that small white object?" he asked.

"It appears to be a head," said Miss Golightly. "Very roughly executed . . ."

"Some sort of fetish, perhaps," said Miss Milton.

Colonel Masters was consulting his papers.

"It doesn't seem to be listed here," he said, "but my brother arranged the exhibits in rather a hurry and he may have omitted some items from the lists."

"Definitely South African workmanship," said General Moult. "No doubt of that at all."

General Moult had served in the South African war and, for that reason, considered himself an authority on every branch of South African culture.

"Perhaps it's one of those human heads that savages treat in a special way," said Miss Milton.

GENERAL MOULT WAS PEERING WITH DIM, SHORT-SIGHTED EYES AT THE MASKS. "WHAT'S THAT SMALL WHITE OBJECT?" HE ASKED.

"They boil them down or something," said Miss Thompson vaguely.

"That's Borneo, not South Africa," said Miss Golightly.

"It must have some bearing on the art or life of South Africa," said Colonel Masters, "or my brother would not have included it. Part of a witch doctor's equipment, no doubt."

"Perhaps the witch doctor used it for telling people's bumps," said Miss Thompson. "It's got a name . . ."

"Phrenology," said Miss Golightly," but I hardly think so."

"I had a curious experience with a witch doctor once," began General Moult and the crowd melted quickly away. They had heard General Moult's stories till they almost knew them by heart.

Archie was left alone in front of the table. His eyes, fixed on the head, grew wider and wider. His mouth dropped open. Bewilderment and dismay chased each other over his features. He had come to the exhibition hoping to get a line on Neo-primitive art, and there—staring at him from its blank eyes—was the head he had left in the hole outside the Post Office. It was battered and disfigured, but there was no mistaking it. It was the head.

He heard a sharp intake of breath and turned to see Ethel standing by him. Ethel's eyes, too, were fixed on the head. The expressions that chased each other over her features were those of horror and fury. The base on which the head was set was so small that the Outlaws had not even noticed it, but Ethel saw the letter E, faintly but unmistakably inscribed, followed by the indecipherable squiggle by which Archie always indicated her name. Moreover, by the side of the name was—again faint but unmistakable—the acorn which, as Archie had confided to her, he intended to be the distinguishing mark of his work. And—to make matters even worse—the face, battered and disfigured though it was, bore a distinct resemblance to Ethel's . . . It might have been a clever and diabolically cruel caricature.

"How *dare* you!" she said under her breath.

Archie goggled.

"I didn't . . ." he said wildly. "I swear I didn't . . . I couldn't . . . I don't know how . . . I never . . . It can't be . . . It isn't . . . it——"

"I've never been so insulted in my life," said Ethel. "I shall never speak to you again as long as I live. Get out of my way."

She went from the french windows down the drive to the gate. Archie followed her, expostulating frantically in a voice that grew higher and higher, squeakier and squeakier. At the gate Ethel turned to him and addressed him with icy dignity.

"If you don't go away at once," she said, "I shall call the police."

Slowly he made his way up the drive again to the house. He could no longer escort Ethel to and from the Village Hall for her Country Dancing class on Wednesday evenings. She had made that only too clear. His Wednesday evenings would be free. He could join the Neo-primitive class at Hadley Art School. Beneath his bewilderment and dismay stirred a half-guilty sense of relief. Rosy visions danced before his eyes. "The outstanding picture in this exhibition was Archibald Mannister's——" "Archibald Mannister, the well known Neo-primitive artist." "It was as a Neo-primitive painter that Archibald Mannister first made his reputation. He——"

Four boys passed him carrying something in a satchel. They called a greeting but he did not even hear it as he neared the house. "At Sotheby's yesterday an Early Archibald Mannister went for three hundred guineas..." But first he must solve the mystery of the head. Had some unscrupulous dealer deliberately stolen it? He entered the library and made his way through the crowd to the table where the witch doctors' masks were displayed. Again his eyes widened and his mouth dropped open.

The head had gone.

The members of William's form sauntered one by one into the classroom. William, Henry, Ginger and Douglas took their seats together in the back row. With blank expressionless face William drew the head from its bag and placed it on the desk in front of him. He had given it a "good wash". Seizing the opportunity when his mother was out of the house, he had plunged it into boiling water with a heavy application of detergent and had scrubbed it as hard as he could with the kitchen scrubbing brush. Every vestige of its features had been removed, leaving an off-white irregularly-rounded ball. Victor Jameson threw it a careless glance.

"What's that?" he said. "A fossilised turnip?"

William looked at the head with renewed interest. The idea intrigued him. Shorn of its features, the thing certainly bore a stronger resemblance to a fossilised turnip than to any part of a statue.

"Uh-huh," he said nonchalantly.

Hubert Lane gave a derisive chuckle.

"I bet Mr. Mostyn will think my map's the best of the whole lot," he said.

"Mr. Mostyn's not coming," said Frankie Parker. "Mr. French is back. I've just seen him. He got over his op. in good time an' Mr. Mostyn's gone to be an actor."

It was true. Mr. French had made an unexpectedly quick recovery and Mr. Mostyn, who in any case considered himself wasted in the teaching profession, had transferred his gifts and his person to a small but exclusive repertory company that specialised in performing "experimental" drama to a limited audience of left-wing intellectuals.

"Well, I expect Mr. French'll like it best," said Hubert. "I——"

Mr. French entered the room and threw a tight mirthless smile around.

"Good morning, boys," he said. "I hope you've profited by these long weeks of leisure. Let us see how much—if anything—you remember." He went to the blackboard and chalked up some columns of figures. "Copy that down and work it out."

"Please, sir, what about the holiday task?" said Hubert.

Mr. French's brows shot together.

"What holiday task?" he growled.

"Mr. Mostyn set us a holiday task, sir," said Hubert.

"To find objects of local interest," said Frankie.

Mr. French uttered a sound expressive of irritation and disgust.

"Well, well, well, well," he said. "Show them to me quickly and get it over."

He strode along the lanes between the desks. the

scowl still heavy on his brow. He waved aside Victor's flint, Peter's coin, Hubert's map, Frankie's oyster shell, Jimmy's photograph, with snorts of exasperation and impatience. At last he came to the Outlaws and stared, startled for a moment, at the head.

"What on earth's that?" he said.

"It's a—a fossilised turnip, sir," said William.

The irritation that Mr. French had—more or less successfully—managed to suppress during the last few minutes suddenly burst its bounds.

"Any more of your impertinence, my boy," he said, "and I'll give you something you won't forget in a hurry. I shall confiscate this—whatever it is—and I warn you that it's no use asking me to return it."

He caught up the head, strode to the desk, put the head inside, then fixed a suspicious look on William.

"What are you grinning at, boy?" he said.

"Nothin', sir," said William, hastily composing his features into their expression of blank imbecility.

He had been enjoying the reflection that, though divested of its more potent magic, the head might still have a few pleasant little practical jokes to play on Mr. French in the course of the next few days.

Then, returning with something of relief to normal life, he began to copy down the sum from the blackboard.

V

WILLIAM AND THE PROTEST MARCHERS

At first William did not notice the girl in the blue dress who was sitting by the roadside. His thoughts were occupied by the circus that was due to arrive at Marleigh the next day. His imagination was a riot of acrobats and clowns, performing bears, prancing horses, daring riders, towering elephants, playful sea lions. But a second glance at the girl roused his interest. Her attitude—elbows on knees, head drooping between hands—was eloquent of weariness and despair. On one side of her was an open attaché case, on the other a little pile of papers. As he stopped to watch her, a gust of wind blew one of the papers across the road. He retrieved it and put it with the others, then continued his silent, scowling scrutiny of her.

"What do you want?" she said at last irritably.

"Nothin'," said William.

She might be a spy, he thought, collecting information about the neighbouring aerodrome, or a nature writer collecting information about the way birds and flowers and things carried on, or someone giving free samples of something.

"Are you givin' anything away?" he said.

"What do you mean, giving anything away?" she snapped.

"Well, once someone came round givin' free packets

"WHAT DO YOU WANT?" SHE SAID IRRITABLY.

of cereal," said William. "I'd rather have some sherbet if you've got any."

"Well, I haven't," said the girl.

"What are you doin', then?" said William bluntly.

The girl looked at him. William was not a handsome child, but something about his rough-hewn, scowling countenance inspired confidence.

"I'm in an awful hole," she said.

"What sort of a hole?" said William. "I often get in 'em, too. I bet I can help you out of it."

"Indeed you can't," said the girl. She took up one of the papers and handed it to him. "Look at that."

He turned his gaze on to it and his scowl grew deeper.

"Gosh!" he said. "What's it mean?"

"It means what it says," said the girl wearily. "You can read, I suppose."

The sheet of paper consisted of several columns. In the first one was printed a list of words: Nato, Unesco, Common Market, Atlantic Alliance, Racial Segregation, Atomic Energy and others that were equally unintelligible to William. The other columns were headed by the words: Very Useful, Useful, Not Useful, Doubtful, Indifferent, and at the bottom of the paper was a line for signature.

"Looks dotty to me," said William.

"It is," said the girl. "Of course it is . . . but I want the job and I'll never get it now."

"But what *is* it?" said William.

"Can't you see?" said the girl. "It's one of those research things. People have to put ticks against all these things to show whether they like them or not."

"Why?" said William.

"So that we can know what people think."

"What does it matter what people think?" said William.

"I just don't know," said the girl after a moment's consideration.

"Why are you doin' it, then?" said William.

"Well, I want to get a job on a research team. You call at people's houses and they put ticks and sign their names." She sighed. "Or else they don't."

"Well, if you want to do it, what's wrong with it? Why aren't you enjoyin' it?"

"Everything's wrong with it," said the girl. "It's just one of those days when nothing goes right. You see, I'm on approval for this day and if I don't get any results I won't get the job and if I do I will."

"Well, why aren't you gettin' 'em?" said William.

"I told you," said the girl. "Because it's one of those days when nothing goes right. People won't listen to me. They just say they're busy and shut the door in my face. They won't even *look* at the papers."

"It's washin' day, of course," said William thoughtfully. "Everyone's a bit like that on washin' day. They wake up in funny tempers. Even my mother does."

"Oh well, it can't be helped," said the girl "Anyway, I've walked and walked till I'm worn out. I can't go another step. Oh dear! I'm so miserable."

Her eyes filled with tears and she dropped her head on her arms.

William's reputation for toughness was beyond question, but there was a hidden streak of chivalry in him that occasionally—very occasionally—found its way to the surface. It found it now. He laid a grubby hand on her shoulder.

"Don't you worry," he said. "I'll find people to sign 'em for you."

She raised brimming eyes.

"Oh, you couldn't," she said. "You *couldn't*!"

"I *could*," said William, his decision hardening in face of her mistrust. "'Course I could. A little thing like that's nothin' to me. It won't take any time at all. I'll go 'n' find people now."

The girl opened her mouth to protest but already William was walking briskly down the road. Once round the bend that hid him from the girl's sight, he slackened his pace. Not for the first time in his young life he realised that he had undertaken a task that might well prove to be beyond his powers. He held a mental review of the inhabitants of the village—Miss Milton, Mrs. Monks, General Moult, Mrs. Bott, Mrs. Barlow, Miss Thompson.... His drooping figure straightened itself. He quickened his step. Miss Thompson.... She was vague and absent-minded and incredibly good-natured. She could never bring herself to turn anyone away from her door. It was almost a physical impossibility for her to say "no". She would sign the paper without question and her signature would encourage others to sign.

With rising hopes he made his way to Miss Thompson's cottage and stood at the gate looking over her garden. It was a pleasant little garden with a lily pond in the centre, rose-beds along the sides, and a herbaceous border at the end. Today it wore an unusually festive air, set out for tea with little tables and chairs, cups and saucers, plates, biscuits and cakes. Evidently Miss Thompson was giving a party. He must get the thing settled before the guests arrived. There was no time to lose.

He approached the front door. It stood open. He gave a series of resounding blows on it with the knocker. Miss Thompson emerged from the kitchen. She looked unlike her usual placid self. Her hair was dishevelled, her face flushed. Even her neat starched apron seemed to hang awry.

"I don't know what you've come about, William," she said, "but I can't attend to you now."

"I only came to ask you to write your name on a

piece of paper," said William. "You needn't bother with the ticks. I'll put 'em in later."

"I don't know what you're talking about, dear," said Miss Thompson.

"I'm talkin' about racin' congregations an' atomic alliances an' a word that's a bit like unicorn but not quite an' a lot more things I've forgotten the names of. I'll get this paper from this girl an' I'll do the ticks for you an'——"

"Will you please go *away*, William," said Miss Thompson. "I've got enough on my mind without you bothering me like this."

Reluctantly William brought his mind from his own problems to Miss Thompson's.

"I know. I mean, I can see you're havin' a party——"

"I'm *not* having a party," said Miss Thompson in a tone of desperation.

"Well, it *looks* like a party," said William. "Anyway, you've got people comin' to tea with you, haven't you?"

Miss Thompson shrugged helplessly.

"I've no idea," she said. "And now will you please *go*!"

She turned to make her way back to the kitchen. William hesitated for a few seconds on the doorstep, then followed her into the kitchen. Preparations for the mysterious party were evidently in train. On the table was a mixing bowl containing some half-whisked eggs and round it stood little piles of currants, sultanas and crystallised cherries.

"Listen," said William, perching on the edge of the table and absent-mindedly putting a couple of crystallised cherries into his mouth. "It won't take me a minute to fetch this paper from this girl an' then all you've got to do is to put your name on it an' you needn't even *think* about the ticks 'cause——"

Miss Thompson had sunk weakly into the nearest chair.

"I'll tell you what's happened, William," she said, "then perhaps you'll understand why I can't possibly attend to anything else just now."

"All right," said William, putting a couple of sultanas into his mouth and settling down comfortably on the table edge.

"It all begins with a society called the Society for the Preservation of Animal Life," said Miss Thompson.

"I sometimes get sick of animals havin' everythin' done for 'em," said William. "They've nothin' to do all day long but jus' sit about an' enjoy themselves. Look at cats."

"This one's against butchers if you know what I mean," said Miss Thompson. "I mean, they don't think we ought to eat them."

"Eat butchers?" said William.

"No, dear. Animals. They don't think we ought to eat beef or mutton or anything like that. They think that cows and sheep and all other animals should be allowed to lead long happy lives with freedom from want and fear and that they should be allowed to attain the peace and dignity of old age and die of simple natural diseases like human beings."

"Dogs are all right," said William, "an' so are some insects. An' I've met guinea-pigs an' goldfish that were quite decent. I shouldn't mind any of them dyin' of natural diseases if they want to. I once had a caterpillar that died when I had mumps an' I bet it caught 'em off me."

"Personally I *like* meat, William," continued Miss Thompson, "and I can't bear nuts or raw cabbage, so there wouldn't be any point in my being a vegetarian. Anyway, when this man came to the door——"

"What man?" said William.

"He was a fat little man with a bald head called Mr. Meggison and he went on talking and talking about this Society and asking me to join it and I'd got a rice pudding in the oven that had been there too long already and I wanted to take it out so I joined the society and gave him half a crown just to get back to the rice pudding and I thought that would be the end of it."

"And wasn't it?" said William, giving a crystalilsed cherry a rudimentary face with pieces of dismembered currant, then consigning it to his mouth. "Wasn't it?"

"No, dear," said Miss Thompson. "He rang me up the next day and said that he hadn't had time to make any more calls in the neighbourhood, but would I form a branch here—enrol members and collect subscriptions and send them up to Headquarters each year."

"Well, I bet it was easy enough formin' a Society in this place," said William. "There's dozens of them already for doin' things an' not doin' things an' stoppin' things an' startin' things. Ginger's mother belongs to seven. One more wouldn't make any diff'rence. I bet you found it easy enough to get people to join it."

"But, William, I *couldn't*," said Miss Thompson earnestly. "I *tried*. I got as far as people's garden gates and I learnt by heart what I'd planned to say to them and I couldn't go in and say it. I just haven't the courage for that sort of thing. Then I thought I'd wait till people came to collect subscriptions from me for *their* societies. But somehow I couldn't do it even then. The words stuck in my throat."

"I once got a piece of chewin' gum stuck in mine," said William. "I forgot I'd got it in my mouth an' tried to swallow it." He took hold of the egg whisk and began to manipulate it with a mixture of absent-mindedness and abandon. "What happened next?"

Miss Thompson gently removed the egg whisk from William's hand and mopped up a few pools of egg from the table.

"Well, he kept telephoning me to ask if I'd formed the branch yet, and—and I couldn't go on saying 'no', William. I just couldn't. So in the end I did a dreadful thing. I simply don't know how to tell you what I did."

"I've done some pretty bad things myself," said William. "Once I got up in the middle of the night and ate a whole raspberry jelly that my mother'd made for the next day."

"It was wrong of you, dear," said Miss Thompson, "but mine was much worse."

"What did you eat?" said William.

"Nothing, dear. I mean, it was about this branch. I pretended that I'd formed this branch. I pretended that I'd got members for it and I invented their names and addresses and I sent up two and six a year from each of them just as if they'd been real people. I did it just to stop him worrying me."

"That was jolly clever of you," said William, impressed. "I bet I couldn't have thought of anythin' better than that myself."

"No, dear, it was wrong. It was very wrong. It was

living a life of deceit and I've been living it for three years and now judgement has fallen on me."

"How?" said William.

"He's coming over today to meet the branch and address it and there isn't any branch for him to meet or address."

William looked out of the window.

"But you've got chairs an' tables an' food set out for them."

"That's the dreadful part, William. Mr. Meggison's sent them down. They send tables and chairs down from Headquarters to the places where they're holding garden meetings, and he sent the food, too, because there was a lot left over from a place where they had a garden meeting yesterday. It's odd"—a far-away look came into her eyes—"but somehow they seem quite real to me, all these people I've invented—Mr. Coleman, Mr. Flower, Mr. Beauchamp, Miss Poppins, Mrs. Belmont and the rest. As soon as I knew about the branch meeting, I started making this cake because I thought that Mrs. Belmont would like it. I've always imagined her a wonderful cook . . . but, of course, there isn't any Mrs. Belmont so it's no use making a cake for her, and—— Oh dear! I shall be publicly disgraced and humiliated. It's false pretences and there's no getting away from it. My knowledge of the law is limited, but I'm sure it's a legal offence and I shall probably get put in prison for it."

''I'll try 'an' get you out if you are," said William. "I've thought of some jolly good ways of gettin' people out of prison."

"That's very kind of you, dear, but I should probably be recaptured even if you did. . . . You'd better go now, I think. I've forgotten what you came about. . . ."

"About you writin' your name on a piece of paper about unicorns an' atomic congregations. . . . You will, won't you?"

"Certainly, dear, if it would give you any pleasure," said Miss Thompson. She gazed dreamily into the distance. "Somehow I feel that I really know them—Mr. Coleman, Miss Poppins, Mr. Beauchamp and the rest. I have no very definite picture of them in my mind but I'm sure I should recognise them if I saw them. . . ."

"I'll go 'n' get the papers," said William.

He ran down the lane to the spot where he had left the girl in the blue dress.

She was still there. But she was not alone. A young man sat by her. They were talking earnestly together.

"I've found one person to write her name on it," announced William breathlessly.

"Go away," said the young man.

"An' I bet I can get more once I've got this one," said William.

"Go away," said the young man again.

The papers were still in the open attaché case. William took a handful, thrust them into his pocket and set off once more for Miss Thompson's cottage. But at the end of the lane he stopped. A ragged little procession was coming down the road. At the head walked a young man with a luxuriant black beard and a red shirt. He carried a notice, fixed on to a wooden post: "Hands off Hannah", and led by a leather lead a plump young pig who ambled dejectedly along uttering short morose grunts at intervals. Behind him

"ARE WE ON THE ROAD TO LONDON?"

straggled a collection of youths and maidens, long-haired, tight-jeaned, wearing brightly coloured scarves and sweaters.

The bearded man also stopped and turned a searching gaze on William.

"Where are we?" he asked.

"He means, are we on the road to London?" said a girl with a tow-coloured fringe that almost hid her eyes.

"Gosh, no!" said William. "You're goin' in the wrong d'rection for London."

The girl flung out her arms in a gesture of exasperation and turned to the bearded man.

"I *told* you, Cedric!" she said. "We're *miles* out of our way."

"It's not my fault, Constantia," said the bearded man with dignity. "It's the fault of that blithering idiot Ferdinand," and he pointed an accusing finger at a tall thin man in lederhosen and an alpine hat. "He definitely undertook to bring the map."

"I can't think how I came to leave it behind," said the man. "As a matter of fact I distinctly remember putting it in my rucksack."

"You can't if you didn't," said a girl in tartan trews with close-cropped ginger hair. "You can't remember a thing you haven't done."

"The memory, I admit, Dolores, may refer to some previous occasion. I naturally pack a map whenever I set out on a hike——"

"You can hardly call this a hike," put in the bearded man aloofly.

"What is it, then?" said William, unable to restrain his curiosity any longer.

They turned to look at him.

"I think we had better tell him the whole story," said Cedric. "We are suffering considerable inconvenience—almost persecution—for our principles, and I think it is our duty to hand on those principles to the younger generation."

"All right. Anything for a bit of a rest," said the girl in tartan trews, going to the road verge and seating herself on the top rung of a stile. Several of the others followed her. The rest formed a circle round Cedric and William.

"Do you believe in freedom?" said Cedric, fixing a piercing gaze on William.

"Yes," said William bitterly, "but I never get any. Gosh! Goin' to school five days out of every seven. *Five* out of every *seven*. It's worse than prison. They don't do sums in prison, an'——"

"Never mind that," said Cedric, cutting him short. "Now listen. We"—he waved his arm in an eloquent gesture that included William, the pig, the group around him, and the group that had draped itself disconsolately on the rungs of the stile—"are students. Undergraduates of Newlick University. You've heard, of course, of Newlick University?"

"No," said William. "Me an' Ginger are Oxford and Cambridge turn and turn about for the boat race an'——"

Again Cedric cut him short.

"Oxford and Cambridge!" he said contemptuously. "Those moth-eaten decayed relics of antiquity! No, ours is the University of the Future. It was only completed last year. We are the first students and a heavy load of responsibility rests on our shoulders."

"Oh, get on with it, Cedric," moaned the girl in the tartan trews, "and then let's *do* something."

Cedric threw her a crushing glance.

"I am trying to hand on the torch to the younger generation, my dear Dolores," he said. "Don't you call that *doing* something? Kindly refrain from interrupting." He turned again to William. "As undergraduates of a new university we have traditions to build up, principles of freedom to inaugurate and maintain. We have no use for the outworn traditions of the older universities. We are determined to build up our own traditions and defend them—defend them——"

"To the death," said a stocky little man who bore a strong resemblance to Dopey in 'Snow White'.

"Exactly. We have a mascot." He pointed to the pig. It raised bleary eyes to his and snorted contemptuously.

"Hannah?" said William, regarding the animal with interest.

"Hannah," said Cedric. "The father of one of our students had a farm and he gave us a piglet. It was to be one of the great traditions of our university—the piglet mascot. We each lent a hand towards its housing and upkeep. We made a little thatched cottage for its home. We made a leather collar with its name on in beaten silver. We fed it on the latest scientific principles and kept it scrupulously clean."

He paused.

"Well, what happened then?" said William.

Cedric bent a sorrowful gaze on Hannah.

"She grew," he said. "We were not prepared for the speed with which she attained maturity. She outgrew her little cottage. She broke out of it one evening and went into the principal's private garden and ate his lettuces."

"Not to speak of his cabbages," said Ferdinand.

"And his purple-sprouting broccoli," said Constantia.

"She broke his garden frame."

"And made hay of his rockery."

"She uprooted his prize delphinium."

"She ran amok."

"Anyway, after that the principal forbade animal mascots."

"Understandable up to a point."

"But an infringement of our liberty. An intolerable infringement of our liberty. It may seem a trivial matter to you but it's the thin edge of the wedge . . . and it's our solemn duty towards unborn generations to resist it. As the first students of Newlick University we have not only to originate tradition but to uphold it."

"You said all this at the Debating Society," said Ferdinand, smothering a yawn.

"And I cannot say it too often," said Cedric with spirit. "The pig tradition set us apart. As far as I have been able to ascertain, none of the dyed-in-the-wool, moth-eaten, older universities have the pig mascot tradition. We have originated it and we must uphold it."

"To the death," said Dopey.

"Yes, but what are you goin' to do about it?" said William, deeply interested in the situation.

"Can't you *see* what we're doing?" said Cedric haughtily. "We're staging a protest march. Our original intention was to march to London and lay our case before the Minister of Education but we started late and—well, I must admit that Hannah has not been co-operative."

"She was sweet in her little house when she was a piglet," sighed Constantia.

"Exactly," said Cedric, "but, of course, conditions on a protest march are different. I suppose that actually she's not accustomed to marching—much less marching long distances. Pulling her along is a tiring business and—to make matters worse—that moron"—he darted another fierce look at Ferdinand—"forgot to bring the map. We tried to take a short cut to join the main road and evidently it took us in the wrong direction. A good many of the marchers have dropped out. These"—he waved his arm round the group—"are the sole survivors. Their names will go down in the annals of the university."

"Cold comfort for the moment," said Dolores bitterly.

"We have, of course, reconsidered our programme," said Cedric, assuming his air of detached dignity. "We intend now to go to the nearest town and lay our case before the educational authorities in that town and perhaps persuade the Press to take the matter up. Which is the nearest town?"

"Hadley," said William, "but it's early closing day an' anyway Ethel—that's my sister—has gone out with the Press in his car an' they won't be back till after tea."

"I'd give my soul for a cup of tea," moaned Constantia.

"It's certainly an idea," said Cedric. He turned again to William. "Is there any sort of café in this village?"

"There's Mr. Bentley's," said William, "but he only

sells ice-cream an' raspberry fiz an' coconut wizards. They're smashing an' the coconut wizards only cost threepence an' the raspberry fiz twopence."

"No, no!" said Constantia with a shudder. "It's *tea* I want."

Suddenly William remembered Miss Thompson's garden—the tables and chairs set out so invitingly, the biscuits, the little cakes, the non-existent members of the non-existent branch.

"I b'lieve I know somewhere where.... Jus' wait a minute. I'll go 'n' see. I'll be back in a minute."

He turned and went quickly down the road to Miss Thompson's cottage. Things there were just as he had left them, except that Miss Thompson looked even more harassed and distraught. She was cutting mountains of bread and butter at the kitchen table. A large kettle was boiling on the gas cooker.

"I don't know why I'm doing this, William," she said. "It's just that I can't stop, if you know what I mean. The whole thing's gone to my head. I just must be doing *something* or I'll go mad. I can't just sit and wait to be publicly unmasked and disgraced. Mr. Meggison may be here any moment now, and, of course, I may be in prison by this very evening. I know so little of the law." She stopped and stood looking dreamily into the distance, the bread knife poised in her hand. "The odd thing is that I still half believe in them, you know —Mr. Coleman, Mr. Flower, Mr. Beauchamp, Miss Poppins, Mrs. Belmont and the rest. I shouldn't be a bit surprised if I looked out at the gate and saw them all trooping in...."

Sue turned her eyes to the window and stood paralysed by amazement, eyes and mouth wide open. The bread knife dropped from her hand. She grabbed hold of William's arm.

"William! Look! *Look!* There they are!"

William's eyes followed hers. There they were—the undergraduates of Newlick University—entering the garden gate. Their longing for tea had overmastered them and they had followed in William's tracks.

"William, they've come to the meeting. Oh, I always *have* believed in miracles. Oh, dear! Oh, dear! It's almost too much.... But I must see about the tea now."

The protest marchers were taking their places at the tables. Cedric had parked Hannah by the herbaceous border. He had stuck the "Hands off Hannah" notice into the soil and tethered Hannah to it by her leather lead. Hannah had sunk on to the ground, abandoning herself, as it seemed, to despair.

"First bit of luck we've had," said Dolores, "running into a tea garden like this just when we were on the point of collapse."

"Funny there was no notice at the gate," said Ferdinand.

"I expect they don't want to attract the riff-raff," said Cedric fastidiously.

Miss Thompson was making tea in her largest teapot, carrying it round the tables, filling the cups, sending William to and fro with plates of bread and butter, basins of sugar, jugs of milk, jars of jam. (Miss Thompson was an inveterate jam maker and jammed fruit all the year round.) An atmosphere of relaxation hung over the little scene. The air was full of a pleasant murmur of conversation. The protest marchers were even beginning to see a certain element of comedy in the situation.

"Just fancy! Marching miles in the wrong direction!"

"Look at old Hannah! I believe she's gone to sleep. We shall have to hire a pram to take her home."

"Smashing strawberry jam, isn't it!"

Then suddenly a car drew up at the gate and a tubby little man, dressed in dark city clothes, descended from it. He opened the gate and walked up the little garden path to the lawn. The protest marchers threw him a casual glance.

"Mr. Meggison!" gasped Miss Thompson.

The impact of reality on her dream world was for a moment almost too much for her. She had a sudden panic impulse of flight but advanced to meet the newcomer with a set bright smile.

"I'm sorry I'm late," said Mr. Meggison. "I had a little trouble with the car." He turned a beaming smile on the protest marchers. "Splendid! Splendid! All the members of our little branch assembled. I congratulate you most heartily, Miss Thompson." His eyes moved on to Hannah, dozing beneath her notice and he rubbed his hands together in delight. "Splendid! Splendid! A truly original touch! Hands off Hannah! A wonderful object lesson of the great principle that we are trying to instil into our fellow beings. Hands off Hannah! Yes, indeed! Why should that beautiful little creature, that exquisitely formed work of nature be sacrificed to man's greed? Hands off her, indeed! I should think so! Well, I mustn't stay long. I have another meeting to attend. I'll just address a few words to your branch."

He took up his stand on the farther side of the pond,

with the pond between him and the marchers, and the herbaceous border behind him . . . and launched into a dissertation on the right of the cow, the sheep, the pig ("Hannah, ha! ha!"), even the humble prawn and winkle to lead full free happy lives unhampered by man's greed.

The protest marchers continued to eat their tea with unabated enjoyment. They didn't know what he was talking about and it didn't seem to matter. The little cakes and scones were delicious. The jam was delicious. The chairs, though hard and on the small side, gave comfort to their aching limbs.

But behind them Hannah was awakening to a sense of her grievances. Till now her life—in her little thatched cottage—had been one of ease and comfort. But today all her finer instincts had been outraged. She had been dragged for miles along a hard hot road. She had not been fed (for the protest marchers, in their zeal, had omitted to bring refreshments for themselves or their mascot). She was tired and hungry, and a dull resentment was smouldering in her breast. She rose to her feet and looked around her.

The herbaceous border was full of fresh green plants. Surely some of them must be edible. She plunged her nose into a bush of lavender and withdrew it with a squeak. A bee, disturbed at its work, had thrust its sting into the tenderest part of her snout. And suddenly dark, age-old forces began to stir in her. Her instincts returned to the dawn of civilisation when, in some primeval swamp, she had charged her enemies and put them gloriously to flight. Mr. Meggison's back was in her direct line of vision, and it seemed to her that this object was the sole cause of her troubles. It was this

HANNAH CHARGED ACROSS THE LAWN AND HURLED HERSELF FULL TILT INTO MR. MEGGISON'S BACK.

object that had brought her, footsore and weary, to this strange place and finally inflicted on her this unendurable pain. With a loud squeak she charged across the lawn and hurled herself full tilt into Mr. Meggison's back.

Mr. Meggison gave a squeak that rivalled hers and fell with a splash into the lily pond. He scrambled out . . . but Hannah, trumpeting her triumph, charged again and tipped him back into the pond before he could recover his balance. And then age-old forces began to stir, too, in Mr. Meggison's breast. He, too, in some primeval swamp had charged and vanquished his foes. He kicked out savagely at Hannah, then seized the wooden post on which her notice had been fixed and which still trailed behind her and began to beat her savagely about the head with it. Cedric joined the fray and Hannah charged this new foe with redoubled violence. He fell against one of the little tables and the table gave way, scattering its contents over the lawn. Then quite suddenly Hannah tired of it all. She returned to her station by the herbaceous border and sank again into a state of apathy.

Miss Thompson was fluttering distractedly around her guests.

"I'm so *sorry*, Mr. Meggison," she panted. "I simply don't know what to do. I mean, I could lend you a dressing-gown while your clothes dried, but it's not really suitable. I mean, it's rather frilly. I bought it in a sale and it's not really *me* . . . but it would at least serve as a covering while . . ."

"No, thank you," said Mr. Meggison. He was soaked from head to foot, but his dignity had not quite deserted him. There was something impressive even in the drops that trickled from his nose. "No, thank you. I will return to my car. I have a raincoat there. It will not take me long to reach home."

Miss Thompson accompanied him down the little path to the road. There was a thoughtful look on her face. A confused and confusing account of the affair by William had solved the mystery of the "branch members" and the sight of the water-logged figure before her gave her an unaccustomed courage and confidence.

"I think, you know," she said gently, "that we shall have to discontinue the branch. The members are all leaving the neighbourhood shortly and my own plans are very unsettled."

Mr. Meggison's tight features relaxed. In his mind was a nightmare picture of himself kicking a young pig, striking it savagely on the head with a stick. . . . The picture would, he knew, gradually fade from his memory, but only if he never again visited the surroundings in which the unspeakable scene had taken place.

"Perhaps you are right," he said judicially. "Small branches in these outlying country places are never very satisfactory. Yes, I think we should do well to close this particular branch. I will send you an official letter, of course, thanking you for your co-operation and the splendid work you have done."

Then gravely, majestically, he dripped his way into his car, raised his hand in a farewell gesture, started the engine and disappeared round the bend of the road.

Miss Thompson returned to the lawn. Her face wore a smile of dreamy happiness. William, who had been an enthralled spectator of the scene, stood by the pond munching biscuits.

"My spirit is freed from a load of guilt, William," she

said. "It's a beautiful feeling. I don't know whether you have ever experienced it."

William considered.

"No, I don' b'lieve I have," he said at last. "I get loads of guilt, all right, but they don't bother me. I get used to 'em."

Cedric approached. He looked bewildered and apprehensive.

"I don't know how to apologise for that unfortunate accident," he said. "If we'd had any idea that it was going to happen we should, of course, have taken precautions. She has always been so even-tempered till today. We feel most mortified that she should have attacked your guest in this unpredictable fashion."

"It's quite all right," said Miss Thompson, giving him a radiant smile. "It's of no consequence whatever."

He glanced at the china scattered over the grass.

"We must at any rate pay for the damage," he said.

"No, no, *no*!" beamed Miss Thompson. "That's of no consequence either."

"Well, we must pay for our tea and——"

"Oh, *no*!" said Miss Thompson. "I shouldn't dream of letting you do that. You must consider yourselves my guests. It's all too complicated to go into now, but you've freed me from a load of guilt and I'm most grateful to you."

Cedric's expression of bewilderment and apprehension deepened. He glanced nervously around.

Hannah still lay by the herbaceous border, uttering short resentful grunts, and on the other side of the hedge the burly, gaitered figure of Farmer Smith could be seen. He was inspecting Hannah with interest.

"Didn't know you were goin' in for pig-keeping, Miss Thompson," he said.

"Oh, it's not mine," said Miss Thompson. "Far from it!" She waved her hand towards Cedric. "It belongs to this gentleman."

Cedric approached the hedge over which Farmer Smith's head protruded.

"Do you know anything about pigs?" he said.

"I do," said Farmer Smith.

"Well, is it possible for a pig to get hydrophobia?"

Farmer Smith wrinkled his brow.

"I've never heard tell of a case," he said.

"Well, this one's been fairly placid till today and today she's had a sort of brain-storm. Charged all over the place, knocked a man into the pond and—well, as you see, made a shambles of the whole place. It seemed to come on quite suddenly. Do pigs ever go out of their minds? Such minds as they have, of course."

"I'll come round and look at her," said Farmer Smith shortly.

"Actually, it's what she stands for, rather than the pig itself that's important to us," said Cedric. "We want to make our mark on our generation, We want our names to be handed down to posterity."

His only audience was William, who stood in front of him still munching biscuits and listening with rapt attention.

"After all," continued Cedric, "what we do in these first few years will set standards and principles for generations yet unborn. My own name," he continued, "may become a household word, among future scholars not only of Newlick University but of—other universities also."

Suddenly William remembered the sheaf of papers that still rested in his pocket. He drew them out.

"May I have your autograph, please?" he said.

Cedric stopped in midstream. Carried away on the swelling tide of his own eloquence, he saw himself as a world-famous figure, a Man of Destiny. It did not seem at all strange to him that this boy should want his autograph.

"Certainly," he said graciously.

He took out his pen and, frowning portentously, scrawled his name with a flourish on the line indicated by William.

Encouraged by this, William approached the other members of the group. Though they had paid scant attention to Cedric's actual words, the general trend of his speech had impressed them. They were the precursors of a new age of liberty and equality. Mascots for everyone. Pigs for all. Like Cedric, they saw nothing strange in William's request. Like Cedric, they signed on the line indicated by William, each on a separate piece of paper.

Farmer Smith continued his examination of Hannah, patting her, soothing her, poking and prodding her.

William thrust the papers into his pocket and, approaching his hostess, took a formal farewell of her, fixing her with the glassy smile that accompanied any exhibition of "manners" on his part and enunciating the words "Thank you for having me" in a loud and husky voice.

"It's been a pleasure, dear," said Miss Thompson vaguely. "You must come again some time when I'm not quite so busy."

William made his way back to the spot where he had left the girl in the blue dress and the young man. They were still there, still talking earnestly together, but obviously on more intimate terms than when he had last seen them. The attaché case still lay open by her side. William placed the papers in it.

The girl threw him a smile over the young man's shoulder, then winked at him. The suggestion of a secret understanding pleased William. He lingered in hopes of improving the acquaintanceship.

"I've jus' been to tea with Miss Thompson," he said. "A pig knocked a man into a pond an'——"

"Go away," said the young man without turning to look at him.

"All right," said William huffily, "if you're not in-t'rested. . . ."

He wandered off down the road in search of Ginger.

Gradually the peace of evening descended on the countryside. In Miss Thompson's garden the chairs and tables and crockery were neatly stacked in the veranda awaiting collection. Miss Thompson stood at her front door making feeble apologetic rejoinders to a man who was trying to sell her an electric polisher. Her pleasant face was overcast. She didn't need an electric polisher. She didn't want an electric polisher . . . but there was a dark foreboding in her heart that at the end of ten minutes—or less—she would have bought one.

The protest marchers were making their way slowly down the Hadley Road. Hannah was no longer with them.

"I think we did the right thing," Cedric was saying. "He said she'd been stung by something and maybe she had, but there was no guarantee that it wouldn't happen again. She might have caused some fatal injury. After all, human life is sacred."

"And he gave us a pretty good sum for her," said Dopey.

"Oh, yes, we haven't done so badly. And if we use the money for some gift to the University that will stamp our names and leave our mark for future generations, the same purpose will have been served. The boy was certainly impressed by the stand we made. He asked for my autograph."

"And mine."

"And mine."

"What about endowing a fellowship?"

"There won't be enough for that, you chump!"

"A bird sanctuary. . . ."

"Don't be daft. A radiogram. . . . "

"Perhaps a few amenities for ourselves. . . . After all, *we* earned the money. . . ."

"Decent old girl who kept the tea gardens, wasn't she? She was evidently impressed by our protest. Wouldn't let us pay a penny."

"A bit on the batty side. She kept calling me Mr. Coleman."

"She called me Miss Poppins."

"Once or twice I got the idea that there was more in the whole thing than met the eye."

"So did I. . . ."

"Well, come on! Let's settle the form our gift will take."

"A clock tower. . . ."

"A bicycle shed. . . ."

"Another drum for the orchestra. . . ."

"I honestly don't know what we quarrelled about," the young man was saying to the girl in the blue dress.

"You were very rude and very unkind," said the girl. "You said I'd never get a job like this. You said I hadn't the guts."

"Well, you'd annoyed me. You seemed to think I wasn't good enough for you."

"Well, you're not, are you?" She waved her hand towards the open attaché case. "It may surprise you to know that all these forms are signed by people in the neighbourhood. What have you to say to that?"

"I eat my words," said the young man. "I apologise. I grovel. You're the world's best research expert. . . . Forgive me and chuck the wretched job and marry me."

She relaxed against his arm.

"If you insist . . ." she said.

William ran Ginger to earth on the outskirts of Crown Wood.

"I've been looking for you everywhere," panted Ginger. "It's come!"

"What's come?" said William.

"The circus."

"I thought it wasn't comin' till tomorrow."

"So did I, but it's *come*. They're settin' it up now. You can see it nearly all through the hedge. There's elephants an' lions an' horses an' bears an' even a monkey that keeps jumpin' about everywhere. . . . I've been lookin' for you for *ages*. What have you been doin'?"

For a moment or two William tried to think what he had been doing but the events in which he had taken part had faded into insignificance beside a circus with elephants and lions and horses and bears and a monkey that jumped about everywhere. . . .

"Oh nothin'," he said impatiently. "Come on!"

VI

THE OUTLAWS AND THE GHOST

"GOSH! Wasn't it awful yesterday?" said William as the four Outlaws walked slowly down the village street.

"Never stopped for a single second," said Ginger.

"Nearly as bad as the one in the Bible," said Douglas.

"Just rained cats and dogs all day," said Henry.

"I wouldn't have minded cats an' dogs," said William. "Cats an' dogs would have been rather excitin'. Gosh! Think of 'em all tumblin' down from the sky!" He gave his short harsh chuckle. "We'd have to have umbrellas made of iron to keep 'em off."

The others considered this picture with rising spirits.

"They'd start fightin' all over the place," said Douglas.

"They'd get caught in the trees," said Henry, "an' we could fetch 'em down."

"They'd come down the chimneys."

"They'd fall into greenhouses an' things."

"My father'd go ravin' mad if one fell into his."

"We could have as many dogs as we liked. I don't think much of cats."

"I'd like a bloodhound for a friend for Jumble," said William.

"He'd make mincemeat of Jumble."

"He would *not*!"

"There might be a special sort of dog without tails an' with ten legs."

They laughed uproariously at this, then Henry returned to the original subject of discussion

"Anyway, it jus' rained without stoppin' from the minute we got up in the mornin' till the minute we went to bed at night. It seemed more like a week than a day. . . . I tried to make a railway bridge with a kit I'd got, but the glue went all over the top of a polished table an' they were mad."

"I tried to catch a wasp with my fishin' net," said Douglas, "an' it got all tangled up in my mother's flower arrangement, an' she was mad, too."

"Yes, an' I had jus' a bit of quiet practice with one of my father's golf balls—'case I take up golf when I'm grown-up—an' it broke the bulb of my father's readin' lamp an' *he* was mad," said Ginger.

"They're always like that on rainy days," said Douglas. "It's funny, but there it is. Every little thing you do seems to make 'em mad."

"I read a book," said William with an air of modest virtue. "My mother promised me sixpence if I'd sit quiet for an hour. I found a book of ghost stories in the bookcase an' I read it."

"Did you get the sixpence?" said Henry.

"Well, I got fivepence halfpenny," said William. "I started talkin' about ghosts in the middle."

"There aren't any ghosts," said Douglas.

"Gosh, there *are*!" said William, his voice rising on a note of protest. "Gosh! You should jus' read that book. There's ghosts on every page."

"Yes, but they were jus' stories," said Ginger.

"They weren't all jus' stories," said William earnestly.

"Some of them were written by the axshul person it happened to. They'd got 'I' all the way through, so it must have been true."

"They're white, aren't they?" said Ginger uncertainly. "An' keep moanin' an' groanin'."

"Not all of 'em," said William. "There's lots of different sorts. One of 'em in this book had joined up with the devil an' went about scarin' people into fits, an' another was the picture of a person in a book—it was an awful creature like a skeleton with yellow eyes an' nails like claws—an' it went on scarin' this man the book belonged to till he had to burn the book to get rid of it, an' there was one about a man that found a whistle an' when he whistled it an awful ole witch came up from under an ash tree where she'd been buried an' nearly killed him."

"Gosh! I'd have kept well out of their way," said Ginger.

"Yes, but you wouldn't always *know* they were ghosts," said William. "There was one in this book that looked like a live person an' acted like a live person an' it wasn't till nearly the end that they found he was someone that had come back after he'd been dead for years."

"Why'd he come back?" said Douglas.

"He'd done a dreadful wrong in his lifetime," said William, "an' he'd got to come back to get it put right. He was a good man at heart but he'd been led astray by evil companions."

"I once read one like that," said Henry solemnly. "His spirit could find no rest an' he'd got to go on walkin' the earth till he'd got this wrong he'd done put right."

"That's how it was with this one" said William.

"What had he done wrong?" said Douglas.

"Well, the one in this book I read," said William, "had got some papers about secret polit'cal information ready to hand over to the en'my, an' he'd hidden them ready to hand over to the en'my an' then he died before he could do it an' after he was dead he repented an' came back to get these papers destroyed. He'd got to walk the earth, same as Henry said, till he'd got them destroyed."

"What did he live on all that time?" said Ginger. "I bet they've not got stomachs, ghosts."

"I tell you, this one *had*," said William. "He was jus' like an ordin'ry man 'cept that he was a ghost. . . . Gosh! I wish I could find one."

"One what?" said Henry.

"A ghost. I've never looked out for one before, but —well, you should jus' read this book. They mus' be all over the place."

Douglas threw a nervous glance around.

"Funny we've never come across any," said Ginger.

"That's 'cause we've not been lookin' out for them," said William. "I bet once we start lookin' out for them we'll find one all right."

"Oh, come on," said Henry impatiently. "I'm sick of talkin' about ghosts. Let's find somethin' interestin' to do."

"There's a new tractor over at Jenks's farm," said Ginger. "It's got some little wheels an' things on that I've never seen before. Let's go an' have a look at it."

"There's a new litter of pigs at Smith's farm," said Douglas. "We might go an' have a look at those."

"We never finished that underground tunnel we were makin' under the stream," said Henry.

"No, an' we're not likely to," said Douglas morosely. "Not at the rate the water keeps pourin' down into it."

"We can have a try," said Henry.

"I'm not goin' to do anythin' else," said William doggedly, "till I've found a ghost. If all the people in that book could find 'em, I don't see why I shouldn't."

They looked at him apprehensively, remembering the strange and unexpected situations into which William's one-track mind had so often led them.

"You might have to go on lookin' for the rest of your life," said Henry.

"They didn't. They found 'em almost on the first page."

"I say! Look at that!" said Ginger excitedly. "It's a Jaguar. Look at its headlights. An' it's got a bonnet that opens as well as a boot."

They stopped to gaze in at the window of the post office—a chaotic medley of provisions, shoes, stationery, articles of clothing, saucepans, crockery and toys—to examine the display of miniature cars that was almost hidden by a pair of Wellington boots.

"It's not got its price on," said William. "Let's go in an' ask how much it is."

They entered the shop beneath an archway of dangling plimsolls, threaded their way past sacks of potatoes and a couple of wheelbarrows to the counter, and stood there discussing the merits and probable price of the Jaguar. The postmistress was at the post office end of the counter, attending to the needs of two women whom William did not know. They were dressed in tweed suits, head-scarves and serviceable brogues.

Their resonant voices cut through the conversation of the Outlaws.

"Have you seen the ghost at Springfield?" said one of them.

"I caught a glimpse of him last night," said the other.

"I think I saw him this morning," said the first, "writing in that little summer-house at the end of the lawn. He was wearing a green beret."

"Come out quick!" whispered William.

They made a dash for the door, leaving behind them a trail of scattered potatoes and overturned wheel-barrows.

The postmistress threw them a glance of mingled resentment and resignation.

"Them boys!" she said with a shrug and continued to dole out stamps and postal orders.

"Did you *hear* her?" William was saying excitedly as they stopped in the street outside the shop. "Didn't I *tell* you! We've found a ghost almost the minute we started lookin' for one."

"We've not found it yet," said Ginger.

"An' we'll prob'ly get in a muddle over it if we do," said Douglas. "Anyway, where's Springfield?"

"It's one of those big houses on the road to Steed-ham," said William. "Oh, come on! Don't jus' stand there *arguin'*. Gosh! We don't want him to vanish before we've seen him, do we?"

"I shouldn't mind," said Douglas.

"P'raps we'd better find out a bit more about it first," said Henry.

"Oh yes, that's right!" said William. "I've taken all this trouble findin' a ghost for you an' all you can do is to stand there *arguin'*!" He flung out his arms in an eloquent gesture. "All right! I'm goin' off to find it an' you can stay here, an' if you never see another ghost for the rest of your lives it'll be *your* fault."

He set off briskly down the street. The others hurried after him, and they walked on together, their slight difference forgotten.

The journey to Steedham across the fields was a short one, enlivened by a further discussion on the subject of ghosts.

"You can see right through 'em," said Ginger. "You can *walk* through 'em."

"Not all of them," said William. "I *told* you about the ghost in this book, didn't I? He was jus' like a real person. He was solid all through, same as you or me, filled right up to the top with bones an' lungs an' things."

"I shouldn't like to *be* one," said Douglas.

"I dunno," said Ginger. "I think it would be rather fun."

"I say! Here we are!" said William, lowering his voice. "Look!"

They had reached an open gate that bore the name Springfield in Gothic lettering. From the gate a short drive led up to a square Georgian house. A shrubbery bordered the drive, and beyond the shrubbery could be seen a neat square lawn and, on the edge of it, a neat square rustic summer-house.

"Look!'" said William excitedly. "There's the summer-house, an' I think I can see someone in it."

Cautiously, keeping well under cover of the shrubs, they made their way towards the summer-house.

"Yes, that's him," said William. "That's the ghost. Look! He's wearing a green beret."

"THAT'S HIM," SAID WILLIAM. "THAT'S THE GHOST!"

A man sat writing at a rustic table in the summer-house. He was young and good-looking but his face wore an expesssion of dejection and ill-humour.

"He's got a guilty look," whispered Henry.

"It's 'cause of this wrong he's done that he's come back to put right," said William.

The young man laid down his pen, took a slab of chocolate from his pocket, broke off a small piece, put it in his mouth, then replaced the slab in his pocket.

"He's got a stomach, all right," whispered Ginger.

"An' he looks solid," said Henry. "I can't see through him."

"Is he vis'ble to all of you?" said William.

They nodded.

"He *mus'* be the sort that's come back lookin' like he did in his lifetime to put some wrong he's done right."

They watched for some moments in spellbound silence. The young man wrote with quick jerky movements. Sometimes he looked up from the paper and the four heads would bob hastily out of sight beneath a laurel bush. Sometimes he would take out the slab of chocolate and absently break off a small piece.

"He's got teeth all right," whispered Ginger. "You can see him chewin'."

"I keep tellin' you," said William irritably, "he's got the *whole* of an inside, same as the one in the book."

"I wonder what he did," said Ginger.

The young man raised his eyes from the paper and the four heads bobbed down again, continuing the conversation among the lower branches of the laurel bush.

"P'raps he robbed a bank."

"Or forged a will."

"Or didn't pay his income tax."

"Or let his motor insurance run out."

"You couldn't put any of those right."

"He's got a nice face but he looks cross."

"He's prob'ly like the one in the book," said William. "Good at heart but led astray by evil companions."

The young man had risen to his feet and was gathering up his papers. Intent on watching his every movement, the Outlaws half rose from their hiding-place, and the young man emerged from the summer-house to find four heads confronting him over the top of a bush.

He smiled.

"Hello," he said. "What's all this? Cowboys and Indians?"

"N-no," stammered William, his eyes still fixed with fearful intensity on the young man's face. "N-no. Not c-cowboys an' Indians."

The young man brought out the slab of chocolate and handed it to them.

"Here! Share it between you—what's left of it."

"Thanks," said William He gulped and swallowed and spoke in a hoarse breathless voice."Are—are—are you a ghost?"

The smile dropped from the young man's face and an expression almost of ferocity took its place.

"I am a ghost—Heaven help me!" he said and strode off in the direction of the house.

"There! He *is* a ghost," said William. "I told you he was."

"He's a jolly decent one," said Ginger. "There's more 'n' half the chocolate left."

"He couldn't have done anythin' really bad," said Douglas.

They divided the chocolate and their voices became somewhat indistinct as they proceeded to discuss the situation.

"It mus' be somethin' to do with this house," said William, "'cause it's this house he's hauntin'." He peered through the laurel bushes. "Yes, he's gone into the house. . . . He's hauntin' it, all right."

Ginger, who had been looking through the small dusty windows of the summer-house, suddenly gave a shout.

"Look! He's left somethin' behind."

He entered the summer-house, picked up a piece of paper from the floor and brought it out to the others. It was a sheet of writing-paper, blank except for one sentence written at the top.

If only I could find the wretched papers and destroy them I could escape.

"Gosh!" breathed William. "That *proves* it. It's jus' the same as that man in that book. He'd got some secret polit'cal papers to give to the en'my, an' then he repented after he'd died an' came back to put it right an' now he wants to get them destroyed an' we've got to help him."

"There isn't any en'my now 'cause there isn't any war," said Ginger.

"There's people that might turn en'mies any minute," said William darkly, "so I 'spect it was one of those he was goin' to give them to."

"Why can't he jus' destroy them himself?" said Douglas.

William considered this for a few moments in silence.

"I 'spect he's forgot where he hid them," he said. "Well, he said he couldn't find them in that paper, didn't he? Prob'ly ghosts lose their mem'ries when they come back. They've got stomachs an' bones an' things but they've not got mem'ries. So we've got to help him."

"Yes, but how?" said Ginger.

William drew his brows together in the ferocious scowl that always accompanied his moments of mental exertion, then the scowl cleared.

"First of all we've got to find out about the people that live in this house he's hauntin'," he said. "'Course, this ghost may've lived here hundreds of years ago. There's no proof when he lived."

"His clothes weren't historical," said Henry.

"Well, everyone'd be starin' at him if he started walkin' about in historical clothes. I expect ghosts can dress up in any clothes they like.... Anyway, we'll find out from our fam'lies about the people who live in this house an' we'll meet in the old barn this afternoon an' make a plan."

The four met immediately after lunch in the old barn. All had managed to collect some pieces of information about the inhabitants of Springfield.

"A man called Mr. Raglan lives there now," said William. "He's written a book called *Hedge of Thorns* that's made him famous. No one likes him, but he's famous, all right."

"An' he inherited the house from his uncle," said Ginger. "His uncle used to live there before Mr. Raglan."

"Yes, an' his uncle was called Alec Merrivale," said Henry, "an' *he* wrote books, too, an' jolly good ones."

"My mother says writin' runs in fam'lies," said Douglas.

"An' this Mr. Raglan's writin' his autobiography now," said Henry.

"What's that?" said William.

"The story of his life," said Henry.

"Oh," said William with interest. "That's not a bad idea. I've a good mind to write mine soon as I get a bit of time."

"Well, where does this ghost come in?" said Ginger.

"He mus' have lived there before that Merrivale man," said William, "an' it was then he got these polit'cal papers an' hid 'em."

"They'll be a bit out of date by now," said Henry.

"They might not be," said William. "They might be future inventions he'd got hold of. . . . Anyway, we've *got* to help him. He's a jolly nice man—ghost, I mean —an' it was decent of him to give us that chocolate."

"I wonder if other people see him besides us," said Ginger.

"Those two women had seen him."

"That only makes six. If only six people can see him it's goin' to be difficult for him to get any help."

"Oh, come on!" said William. "He may be doin' somethin' desp'rate while we're wastin' time hangin' about like this."

"Well, he can't kill himself, anyway," said Henry. "I bet that's one of the things a ghost can't do."

"I wish you'd stop talkin' for two *minutes*," said William irritably, "an' let me *think*. . . . Now listen." He drew the paper from his pocket and studied it frowningly. "We've got to find those papers an' destroy them so's he can stop walkin' the earth an' his spirit can find rest."

"How'll we start?" said Ginger.

"First we've got to find out where they're hidden an' they mus' be hidden somewhere in that house 'cause that's the house he's hauntin'."

"It's not so easy, you know," said Douglas, "gettin' into other people's houses an' I bet it'll end in a muddle."

"No, it won't," said William. "I'm jolly good at gettin' into other people's houses. . . . Come on. Let's have a try now."

They set off briskly across the fields to Steedham, slackening their pace as they approached the gate of Springfield. Then silently, in single file, they crept up to the house under cover of the shrubs. A french window stood open on to a terrace at the back of the house. William peered furtively into the room.

"There's no one there," he said. "Come on. . . . We can have a look round, anyway."

Crouching, almost crawling, they crossed the terrace and entered the room by the french window.

"It's all right," said William, looking round. "There isn't anyone. . . . Come on, let's start." He opened a drawer in a small bureau that stood against the wall. "There's nothin' here but envelopes an' ——"

He stopped.

A man had risen from an arm-chair, whose back had been turned to the window, hiding its occupant. He was a stout stocky man with an oily smile and small malicious eyes.

"And what can I do for you, my young friends?" he said.

The envelopes fell from William's hands.

"W-well," he stammered, "we're jus' sort of lookin' for somethin', that's all."

"And what are you looking for?" said the man.

"Jus' some papers," said William, picking up the envelopes and replacing them in the drawer. "Don't bother about us. We—we'll go now. . . ."

"Oh no," said the man, interposing himself between the boys and the french window. "You mustn't run away as soon as you've arrived. I should like an explanation of your visit, you know."

"Are you Mr. Raglan?" said William.

The man bowed in mock politeness.

"I am Mr. Raglan," he said, "and this is my house. Perhaps I might trouble you again for an explanation of your presence here. . . . What exactly are you looking for?"

"Nothin'." said William, maintaining his air of nonchalance with some difficulty. "We jus' sort of got lost. We sort of took the wrong turnin' an' got in here by mistake."

"It's about the ghost," said Ginger. "You see——"

"He gave us some chocolate," said Douglas.

"Shut up!" said William.

"Oh." The man's slow silky voice became slower and silkier. "You like chocolate, do you?"

"Gosh, yes," said Douglas.

"Well, well," said Mr. Raglan, "I'll fetch you some. I have some in my study. One must entertain one's guests. . . ."

He left the room abruptly. The Outlaws looked at each other uneasily.

"I don't like him," said Ginger.

"You were an idiot to tell him about the ghost," said William.

"I thought he might help us find the papers," said Ginger.

"Well, he won't," said William. "You can see that by jus' lookin' at him."

"Let's go away quick before he comes back," said Douglas.

"No, we jolly well won't," said William. "He's actin' jolly suspicious an' I bet he's got somethin' to hide. I shouldn't be surprised if he's one of those evil companions that led this ghost astray."

They wandered aimlessly about the room.

"It's a pretty large house to have to hunt through," said Ginger dispiritedly. "It'll take us *weeks*. . . ."

"Sh!" said William. "He's comin' back."

The door opened and Mr. Raglan reappeared. He held a chocolate box that contained four chocolates. His smile was larger and oilier than ever.

"YOU REALLY OUGHT TO SEE YOURSELVES, YOU KNOW.

"Only four left, I'm afraid," he said, "but it makes one each, doesn't it?"

"Er—thanks," said William, disarmed by this kindly attention. "Thanks very much."

"One each, better than nothing," chuckled the man. "Now put them into your mouth at the word of command. . . . One . . . two . . . three . . . *go*!"

Each of the Outlaws popped a chocolate into his mouth . . . then spluttering, sneezing, gasping, they staggered about the room.

Mr. Raglan watched them with impish glee, chuckling maliciously, rubbing his hands together.

"Ha-ha!" he chuckled. "That'll teach you to respect the laws of property, my young friends! Didn't take me long, did it? Just scooped out the cream from four

IT'S THE FUNNIEST SIGHT I'VE SEEN FOR A LONG TIME."

chocolate creams, mixed it freely—*very* freely—with red pepper—I have a specially pungent variety of red pepper—and plugged it up neatly with a piece of plain chocolate. You really ought to see yourselves, you know. It's the funniest sight I've seen for a long time."

The Outlaws stumbled towards the door.

"One moment!" said Mr. Raglan.

They stopped, irresolute, on the threshold.

"There is a dark cellar beneath this house, and if you ever dare to repeat this exploit you will find yourselves imprisoned there and it is unlikely that your friends will ever set eyes on you again. In years to come, of course, four little skeletons might be discovered, but . . ."

It was a meaningless threat, uttered in a half-joking fashion, but there was malice behind it—malice and intent to terrify the four small boys who confronted him.

"Huh!" spluttered William, infusing—as far as he could—an air of bravado into his spluttering. "Huh! . . . Come on!"

He led the way out of the french window and, once outside the window, still spluttering and choking, they ran across the lawn and out of the front gate. They did not stop till they reached the refuge of the old barn. Their choking and spluttering had by that time somewhat abated.

"Well, what do we do now?" said Ginger.

"Give it up," said Douglas.

"No, we jolly well won't," said William. "He's a villain, all right. We only jus' escaped with our lives. I bet those secret papers are hid in that house an' I bet he knows where they are an' I bet he's goin' to hand them over to the en'my soon as he gets the chance. He was tryin' to poison us 'cause he knew we were on his track."

"It was only pepper," Henry reminded him. "It was jolly beastly, but it was only pepper."

"Pepper!" jeered William. "It was somethin' worse than pepper. I've tasted pepper an' this wasn't jus' pepper. It was poison. I could *taste* the poison in it. We only jus' got out alive."

"An' we can't go back," said Ginger. "He'll be on the look-out for us."

"Y-yes," said William thoughtfully. Then his brow cleared. "But listen! He's havin' a sort of party on Saturday. I heard my fam'ly talkin' about it. It's to mark this book he's written sellin' its fifty thousandth copy or somethin' like that. He's invitin' critics an' publishers and lit'ry people as well as people in the village. I b'lieve *everyone's* goin' to it. He thinks an awful lot of himself jus' 'cause he's written a book. I bet it's not as good as that one I wrote called *The Bloody Hand.*"

"'Course it isn't," said Ginger. "That was a *smashing* book."

"Well, I don't see how any of this is goin' to help," said Henry.

"'Course it's goin' to help," said William. "They'll all be busy with this party. They'll be havin' it in that big room we were in, an' the servants will all be in the kitchen, an' the rest of the house'll be empty. So that's what we'll do. We'll search the house while they're havin' the party. It's a jolly good idea."

The other three looked doubtful.

"He's sure to find us," said Henry.

"An' I don't see what's to stop him poisoning us again," said Ginger.

"I don't think my mother'd like me to do it," said Douglas.

William assumed his air of leadership.

"Well, you're *goin'* to. We're all goin' to. We're goin' to find those papers an' destroy them, an' rescue this ghost from havin' to walk the earth so's his spirit can find rest. An' if you don't want to come, I'll do it myself. I can do it myself easy. I bet they're hidden in the attic. You can't hide things in ordin'ry rooms 'cause someone always finds them, but no one looks for things in attics. I once kept a c'lection of insects in the attic an' no one ever found them till they escaped an' came downstairs. They're full of junk, attics are, an' you could hide secret papers in one for *years*."

Already they felt committed to the plan. Their spirits were rising to meet the challenge of adventure.

"It's worth tryin'," said Henry.

"Huh! I should jolly well think it is," said William. "Now listen." He sank his voice to a whisper and they gathered closely round him. "We'll wait till this party's got started, then we'll go up to the attic and have a good hunt all over it an' I *bet* we find those secret papers. The party starts at six so we'll meet here at quarter to."

They saw the young man twice in the interval before the party. On the first occasion they met him striding over Ringers Hill and he waved to them as he passed.

"He's still walkin' the earth," said Henry, looking back to him sorrowfully.

On the other occasion he passed them on a motorcycle.

"He can ride a motor-cycle," said Ginger with interest.

"P'raps it's a special sort," said Douglas.

"No, I *told* you," said William impatiently. "He's the kind that has bones in his legs, same as you an' me."

They met in the old barn on the evening of the party, made their way over the fields to Springfield, crept up the drive in the shelter of the shrubs, and took up their positions near the house. Through the branches of a thick laurel bush they watched the guests arrive—the London contingent of critics, publishers and writers; the local contingent of Monks, Botts, Miss Milton, General Moult and the rest.

William peered out cautiously from his laurel bush as his parents approached.

"She looks all right," he said with ill-concealed pride. "She's got that hat on that she said made her look like a pineapple, but it looks jolly nice to me."

Ginger, Henry and Douglas also subjected their parents to critical scrutiny as they passed. Douglas's father threw a searching glance in their direction that made them shrink still farther into their hiding-place, but he was merely pointing out that a spindly weigela in the neighbourhood of the laurel had been insufficiently pruned.

Gradually the last stragglers entered the front door of Springfield. The guests could be seen through the window, glasses in hand, moving to and fro . . . chatting . . . greeting each other. A small crowd surrounded a tall thin man with a bald head and bushy eyebrows, and a short squat man with a black goatee beard was holding forth to an earnest-looking group, all of whom obviously belonged to the London contingent. The largest group was clustered round Mr. Raglan, who was smiling his oily smile and waving his plump white hands as he talked. The young man was standing apart from the others, looking morose and detached.

"No one's takin' any notice of him," said Ginger.

"I don't s'pose they can see him," said Douglas.

"Never mind that," said William. "Come on. They're all inside the room now. Let's go up to the attic."

They made their way to a small side door. It was open. In single file, huddling against the wall, they crept along a stone passage . . . and up a narrow back staircase. Voices and the clink of glasses and crockery came from the kitchen regions, but passage and staircase were deserted. Up the stairs to the top storey . . . then up the small steep ladder-like flight of steps . . . and into the attic.

They stood gazing round, wide-eyed with interest. Cardboard boxes, suitcases, trunks, hampers, stringless tennis racquets, old picture-frames, an ancient hip-bath, oil lamps, broken deckchairs, piles of old books and magazines, a phonograph, a punch-ball, a tricycle, a crumbling bird-cage, a dilapidated flour-bin. . . .

Henry began a cautious attack on the punch-ball and Ginger climbed on to the tricycle.

"Stop messing about," said William sternly. "We've got to go through all these boxes till we find those papers."

Reluctantly they left punch-ball and tricycle and set to work on the hunt, emptying box after box, scattering the contents on the floor around them.

"Nothin' here. . . ."

"Rusty old skates...."

"Old curtains an' things...."

"Old photographs...."

"Old books...."

William was becoming somewhat bored by the search. He stood up and surveyed his surroundings. His eyes rested on a roof beam that ran from end to end of the long low room.

"I bet I could swing myself right from one end of this to the other," he said.

"Thought you said 'don't mess about'," grumbled Douglas.

"Well, it won't take a minute an' I'm beginnin' to get stiff, emptyin' boxes. I need a bit of exercise."

He climbed on to an old wicker hamper, clasped the beam with both hands and set off, swinging his way across the room.

"I'm doin' it jolly well," he said exultantly. "I've nearly got to the end. I bet a real acrobat couldn't do it better. I——"

He wobbled precariously, lost his grip with one hand, waved it wildly in the air, lost his grip with the other and fell heavily on to an open suitcase that happened to be just beneath him.

"Well, I've jus' about broken every bone in my body," he said, as he rose from the wreckage and stood rubbing his thighs, "but I nearly did it. I bet I'll do it all right if I try again. I——" He looked down at the broken suitcase and his eyes widened. "Gosh!" His voice sank almost to a whisper. "*Look!*"

They looked down at the suitcase. William's fall had broken the sides but had also evidently released a spring. What had appeared to be the bottom of the case had

"GOSH!" WILLIAM'S VOICE SANK ALMOST TO A WHISPER. "LOOK!"

opened, revealing a secret compartment. And in the secret compartment was a pile of papers.

"The poli'cal papers," gasped William. "The ones he'd hid and forgot where he hid them. . . . They're *here*!"

They fell eagerly upon the papers, taking them out of the suitcase, spilling them over the floor. Each page was closely covered with erratic, almost illegible handwriting. The lines sloped up the pages at an abrupt angle. Whole sections had been crossed out and corrections written and rewritten on every available space.

The Outlaws had each seized a handful of papers and were studying them with frowning concentration.

"Can't read a word," said Ginger at last. "I think it's in some foreign language."

"No, it isn't," said Henry. "It goes into English every now and then. . . . I can read 'geranium' here quite clear."

"It mus' be a code word for somethin' else, then," said William. "*I know*! It's a code for 'uranium'. Well, that *proves* it. It was atom bomb secrets he was goin' to give away an' we've got to destroy them quick so's his spirit can find rest."

"How *can* we destroy them?" said Ginger. "We don't know where the dust-bin is an' even if we put them there someone'd be sure to find 'em an' fish 'em out."

William had climbed on to the wicker basket again and was looking out of the open skylight.

"There's a bonfire down there," he said. "I think it's in a sort of kitchen garden. No one's with it. It's jus' burnin' away by itself. . . . There's no one about. It'll be all right. Come on! Let's take them there now."

They gathered up the papers and William tied them into a loose bundle with a length of string that trailed from an overturned box.

"Come on," he whispered hoarsely, "an' don't make a sound."

Silently, cautiously, their faces tense and earnest, they tiptoed down the stairs and reached the small side door by which they had entered. William stood in the shadow of the doorway, gazing warily around.

"We'll have to go across the lawn to get to the part of garden where the fire is," he said, "but they're all in that room havin' drinks an' things so it should be all right."

Casting fearful glances over their shoulders at the house, they began the perilous crossing.

Suddenly the front door was flung open and a burst of conversation issued from it.

"You must certainly see the garden," they heard in Mr. Raglan's voice. "Especially the herb garden. My uncle made a delightful little herb garden."

William gazed desperately around. There was a beech tree by the edge of the lawn with low-growing branches.

"Let's get up there," he said. "We can stay there till they've gone in again."

The guests had now emerged from the house and were clustered round a rather showy little fuchsia shrub that grew by the front door. Their backs were turned to the Outlaws but there was not a moment to be lost. William bundled the papers under his pullover and began the ascent. The others followed and, when the guests turned from the examination of the fuchsia shrub, the Outlaws were all safely up the tree and the coast was clear.

But not *quite* clear.

For one of the sheets of paper had escaped from the bundle and lay on the ground beneath the tree. The tall man whom the Outlaws had seen through the window at the beginning of the party strolled across to it casually and picked it up. As he read it his brows shot together and his lips tightened. Turning round, he beckoned to the bearded man and together they bent their heads over the sheet of paper.

"It's the first page of the opening chapter of *Hedge of Thorns*," said the tall thin man. "And it's in Alec's handwriting. I was his agent for thirty years and I'd know that hand in a hundred. I'd take my oath to every letter."

"Good Lord!" said the bearded man. "So would I. There's no possibility of doubt. I published all his books, and every page of his typescript consisted largely of corrections. I've spent years of my life wrestling with this fist of Alec's. It's certainly the opening page of *Hedge of Thorns*—but why in Heaven's name is it in Alec's handwriting? Where has it come from? Where's the rest of it?"

As if in answer to his question, a shower of manuscript suddenly descended on him from the branches above. William had made an incautious movement that released the bundle of papers from their insecure mooring beneath his pullover. They fluttered down in the breeze. Guests caught them in their hands or picked them up from the ground with expressions of growing bewilderment.

"Is it a sort of advertisement?" said Mrs. Brown.

"A message from Outer Space, perhaps," said Miss Thompson vaguely.

But the tall thin man and the bearded man were collecting the papers and examining them with expressions that changed from bewilderment to suspicion, from suspicion to grim certainty.

They approached their host. A yellow tinge had invaded Mr. Raglan's countenance. His eyes wore a glazed set look.

"As your publisher, Mr Raglan," said the bearded man, "I should like an explanation of this."

"As your agent," said the tall thin man, "I, too, would welcome enlightenment."

Mr. Raglan's teeth were bared in a ghastly smile.

"Of what?" he gibbered. "I don't understand. I—I——"

The guests had gathered round. The young man stood by Mr. Raglan with a look of interest and curiosity on his face.

"Of this manuscript," said the bearded man. "It is —word for word—the manuscript of *Hedge of Thorns*, which you submitted to me as your own work and which I published under your name early this year. Yet it is indubitably in your uncle's handwriting. Everyone who had any dealings with him would swear on oath that this was his handwriting."

"I was his agent," said the tall thin man, "and certainly I would swear to his handwriting in a court of law."

"We are waiting for your explanation, Mr. Raglan."

Mr. Raglan's face grew yet more yellow, his eyes more glazed, his lips more fixed in their nightmarish grin. Drops of perspiration stood out on his brow.

Then suddenly a commotion arose from behind them and they all turned to see four boys slithering down the tree.

"Heavens above!" groaned Mr. Brown. "It's William."

But William was making his way to the group round Mr. Raglan. He had not caught the words but he felt that the moment for intervention had arrived.

"I can 'splain," he panted. "It's nothin' to do with

Mr. Raglan." His finger shot out in the direction of the young man. "It's *him*."

Mrs. Brown started forward in anguish, but her husband laid a restraining hand on her arm.

"Ignore him," he said. "Forget you ever had a younger son."

"Oh, but I did," wailed Mrs. Brown, "and the poor boy's out of his senses."

"He never had many to be out of, my dear," said Mr. Brown. "Let's go and inspect the fuchsia again. I feel a sudden overpowering interest in the plant."

The guests were staring at William—the faces of the London contingent in frozen amazement, the faces of the locals in weary resignation. . . . William Brown at the bottom of every piece of mischief, as usual.

William had pushed his way to the front of the group. The undergrowth of the shrubbery, the dust and cobwebs of the attic, the lichen of trunk and branches, had left plentiful marks on his person. His hair was dishevelled, his tie askew, his pullover torn, his features barely discernible, but his face was set and purposeful as he pointed a grubby finger at the young man.

"It's him," he repeated. "It's the ghost. He's got to go on walkin' the earth till he's set this wrong right." His grubby finger now indicated the pile of manuscript in the publisher's hands. "It's got to be burnt so's his spirit can find rest."

"My dear boy," said the publisher, "I see no ghost."

"No, p'raps you don't," said William. "We can see him but I don't s'pose everyone can. He wrote these secret papers in his lifetime." The young man's jaw had dropped open. "They're about atom bombs. He wrote them for the en'my then repented an' they've got to be destroyed."

"He meant no harm," said Ginger.

"He was led astray by evil companions," said Henry.

Suddenly the general interest was directed elsewhere. For Mr. Raglan was quietly and unobtrusively sloping off. Probably he did not himself know where he hoped to slope off to, but it was evident that he was driven by an irresistible urge to escape from his present surroundings.

"Quick!" called the tall thin man. "Stop him!"

Mr. Raglan was nimbler than he looked. Already he was well on his way to the garage where his large Daimler stood by, as if waiting to take part in his escape. The two men set off after him. Some of the guests joined in the chase. William was starting forward to follow them when the young man laid a hand on his shoulder.

"One moment!" he said. "Now will you kindly tell me what all this is about?"

The Outlaws and the young man were in the attic among a chaos of upturned boxes and their scattered contents. The shouting and the tumult had died. Host and guests had departed. Only the young man had stayed behind to sort out the situation with the Outlaws and inspect the scene of the discovery. He sat on the upturned flour-bin and the Outlaws on the floor around him. Introductions had been performed and it turned out that the young man was no ghost but an ordinary mortal called Nicholas Bolton.

"You see," he was saying, "this Raglan chap had come across the manuscript of a novel that his uncle had written shortly before his death, made sure that no one knew anything about it—his uncle was always very cagey about his work and never told anyone anything about a book till it was ready for publication—and decided to pass it off as his own. He just typed it out—Heaven knows how he managed to decipher the handwriting—and sent it to the publisher. It was rather different from his uncle's usual stuff and no one suspected that it hadn't been written by Raglan."

"They said writin' runs in fam'lies," said Douglas.

"Yes, that helped him to get away with it."

"Why didn't he burn the manuscript?" said William.

"Well, his uncle had left some notes at the end explaining some rather obscure points in the novel, so Raglan kept it for reference in case any questions were raised. He had this suitcase with a false bottom—presumably he'd used it for circumventing the Customs at some time or other—so he hid the manuscript there and thought it would be safe, especially among all this junk."

"What'll happen to him?" said William. "Will he go to prison?"

Mr. Bolton shrugged.

"I don't know anything about the legal side of it. He's gone to see his solicitor now, but the publisher's got the manuscript and I suppose he'll be going to see *his* solicitor. Whatever happens Raglan will be completely discredited."

"His name will be mud to the end of time," said Henry solemnly.

"Exactly."

"I'm sorry for us you're not a ghost," said William regretfully, "but I'm glad for you."

"Yes, it would have been rather a wearing life," agreed Mr. Bolton.

"But you *did* write that about destroyin' papers an' escapin'," said William.

"Oh, yes . . . well, it's rather a long story."

"We don't mind," said William.

"We like 'em long," said Ginger.

"There's lots of time," said Douglas.

"Yes, I suppose so. . . . I'm leaving early tomorrow morning and my packing won't take long."

"An' those women said you were a ghost," said Henry.

"Yes, but they used the word in a special sense. You see, this Raglan chap had got a bit above himself. The success of *Hedge of Thorns* had gone to his head. And people were urging him to write his autobiography. He couldn't write for toffee, but he didn't want to refuse so he engaged another chap to write it for him pretending that he hadn't the time to do it himself. And the man that writes another man's stuff for him is called a 'ghost'."

"But that paper in the summer-house . . ." said Ginger.

"Ah, yes, that was part of a letter I was writing to a friend confiding my troubles. You see, the first man Raglan got to write for him packed up after a week. He could tell that the chap was phoney and the stuff he was drooling out as his life story just didn't hold water. So Raglan got me and tied me hand and foot by a legal agreement to stay with him till the autobiography was written to his satisfaction."

"Gosh!" muttered William.

"I didn't know anything about the other man, of

course, and I'd read *Hedge of Thorns* and admired it tremendously. I was out of a job and thrilled to get this one . . . then I was offered another job that I'd have given my soul to take but I was bound hand and foot to this wretched blighter by the agreement I'd signed. I'd found out by then, of course, how phoney he was and I suspected that the stuff he was pouring out as his life story was pure invention, but he wouldn't release me from the agreement. It was the legal agreement, of course, that I wanted to destroy."

"Can you take the other job now?" said William.

"Oh, yes, I've just been on the telephone about it. I shall have to get moving quickly but I've got it all right."

"What job is it?" said Henry.

"Taking part in an Antarctic expedition."

"Gosh!" breathed William. "An *Antarctic* expedition!"

"Yes . . . I went on one with these same chaps a few years ago and they'd decided on another and wanted me to join them."

"You—you've axshully *been* on an Antarctic expedition?"

"Yes."

"Did you have adventures?"

"Quite a few."

"Oh, tell us."

Mr. Bolton smiled.

"All right." He lit his pipe and settled down as comfortably as he could on the flour-bin. "Where shall I begin?"

"At the beginning," said William.

"Very well. . . . We got to the Weddle Sea all right.

Had a close shave with a glacier and nearly got caught in an icepack . . . then the real stuff began. You couldn't see anything but snow and ice and you could hardly see them for the blizzard. Two of the sledges fell into a crevasse and we thought we were never going to get them out. Then the dogs began to fall sick. . . ."

The four boys sat there, eyes fixed on him, bodies tensed.

The attic, with its store of junk, had vanished. They were out in the snow and ice, the blizzards and gales, lost to everything but the white frozen world of the Antarctic. . . .